I0764564

YOUNG CAPTAIN JACK
or, THE SON OF A SOLDIER

MORE WILDSIDE CLASSICS

Dacobra, or The White Priests of Ahriman, by Harris Burland
The Nabob, by Alphonse Daudet
Out of the Wreck, by Captain A. E. Dingle
The Elm-Tree on the Mall, by Anatole France
The Lance of Kanana, by Harry W. French
Amazon Nights, by Arthur O. Friel
Caught in the Net, by Emile Gaboriau
The Gentle Grafter, by O. Henry
Raffles, by E. W. Hornung
Gates of Empire, by Robert E. Howard
Tom Brown's School Days, by Thomas Hughes
The Opium Ship, by H. Bedford Jones
The Miracles of Antichrist, by Selma Lagerlof
Arsène Lupin, by Maurice LeBlanc
A Phantom Lover, by Vernon Lee
The Iron Heel, by Jack London
The Witness for the Defence, by A.E.W. Mason
The Spider Strain and Other Tales, by Johnston McCulley
Tales of Thubway Tham, by Johnston McCulley
The Prince of Graustark, by George McCutcheon
Bull-Dog Drummond, by Cyril McNeile
The Moon Pool, by A. Merritt
The Red House Mystery, by A. A. Milne
Blix, by Frank Norris
Wings over Tomorrow, by Philip Francis Nowlan
The Devil's Paw, by E. Phillips Oppenheim
Satan's Daughter and Other Tales, by E. Hoffmann Price
The Insidious Dr. Fu Manchu, by Sax Rohmer
Mauprat, by George Sand
The Slayer and Other Tales, by H. de Vere Stacpoole
Penrod (Gordon Grant Illustrated Edition), by Booth Tarkington
The Gilded Age, by Mark Twain
The Blockade Runners, by Jules Verne
The Gadfly, by E.L. Voynich

Please see www.wildsidepress.com for a complete list!

YOUNG CAPTAIN JACK

or, THE SON OF A SOLDIER

HORATIO ALGER, JR.

WILDSIDE PRESS

YOUNG CAPTAIN JACK

This edition published in 2007 by Wildside Press, LLC.
www.wildsidebooks.com

PREFACE.

"Young Captain Jack" relates the adventures of a boy waif, who is cast upon the Atlantic shore of one of our Southern States and taken into one of the leading families of the locality. The youth grows up as a member of the family, knowing little or nothing of his past. This is at the time of the Civil War, when the locality is in constant agitation, fearing that a battle will be fought in the immediate vicinity. During this time there appears upon the scene a Confederate surgeon who, for reasons of his own, claims Jack as his son. The youth has had trouble with this man and despises him. He cannot make himself believe that the surgeon is his parent and he refuses to leave his foster mother, who thinks the world of him. Many complications arise, but in the end the truth concerning the youth's identity is uncovered, and all ends happily for the young son of a soldier.

In its original shape Mr. Alger intended this tale of a soldier's son for a juvenile drama, and it is, therefore, full of dramatic situations. But it was not used as a play, and when the gifted author of so many boys' books had laid aside his pen forever the manuscript was placed in the hands of the present writer, to be made over into such a book as would evidently have met with the noted author's approval. The success of other books by Mr. Alger, and finished by the present writer, has been such that my one wish is that this story may meet with equal commendation.

Arthur M. Winfield.
February 16, 1901.

CHAPTER I.

THE ENCOUNTER ON THE BRIDGE.

"Get out of the way, boy, or I'll ride over you!"

"Wait a second, please, until I haul in this fish. He's such a beauty I don't wish to lose him."

"Do you suppose I'm going to bother with your fish? Get out of the way, I say!" And the man, who sat astride of a coal-black horse, shook his hand threateningly. He was dressed in the uniform of a surgeon in the Confederate Army, and his face was dark and crafty.

The boy, who was but fourteen and rather slenderly built, looked up in surprise. He was seated on the side of a narrow bridge spanning a mountain stream flowing into the ocean, and near him rested a basket half-filled with fish. He had been on the point of hauling in another fish—of extra size—but now his prize gave a sudden flip and disappeared from view.

"Gone! and you made me miss him!" he cried, much vexed.

"Shut up about your fish and get out of the way!" stormed the man on the horse. "Am I to be held up here all day by a mere boy?"

"Excuse me, but I have as much right on this bridge as you," answered the boy, looking the man straight in the eyes.

"Have you indeed?"

"I have."

"Perhaps you think yourself of just as much importance as a surgeon in the army, on an important mission."

"I didn't say that. I said I had just as much right on this bridge as you. It's a public bridge."

"Bah! get out of the way and let me pass. I've wasted time enough on you." The man tugged nervously at his heavy mustache. "Which is the way to Tanner's Mill?"

To this the youth made no reply. Gathering up his fishing rod and his basket, he stepped to the river bank and prepared to make another cast into the water.

"I say, tell me the way to Tanner's Mill," repeated the man.

"I reckon you had better go elsewhere for your information," returned the boy quietly, but with a faint smile playing over his handsome, sunburned face.

"What, you young rascal, you won't tell me?" stormed the man.

"No, I won't. And I beg to let you know I am no rascal."

"You are a rascal," was the snappy reply. "Answer my question, or it will be the worse for you," and now the man leaped to the ground and advanced with clenched fists. Possibly he thought the youth would retreat; if so, he was mistaken.

"Don't you dare to touch me, sir. I am not your slave."

"You'll answer my question."

"I will not."

"Why not?"

"Because you haven't treated me decently; that's why."

"You hold a mighty big opinion of yourself."

"If I do, that's my own business."

"Perhaps you are a Northern mudsill."

"No, I am just as loyal to the South as you or anybody."

"I wouldn't care to take your word on that point, youngster. I am on an important mission, and if you sympathize with our South in this great war you'll direct me to the short way to Tanner's Mill."

"Do they expect a fight at Tanner's Mill?"

"Don't bother me with questions. Show me the road, and I'll be off."

"Keep to the right and you'll be right," answered the youth, after a pause, and then he resumed his fishing.

The man scowled darkly as he leaped again into the saddle. "How I would love to warm you—if I had time," he muttered, then put spurs to his steed and galloped off.

"So he is going to Tanner's Mill," mused the boy, when left alone. "If they have a fight there it will be getting pretty close to home. I don't believe mother will like that."

As will be surmised from the scene just described, Jack Ruthven was a manly, self-reliant boy, not easily intimidated by those who would browbeat him.

He lived in a large mansion, set back some distance from the river, upon what was considered at that time one of the richest plantations in South Carolina.

Mrs. Ruthven was a widow, having lost her husband, Colonel Martin Ruthven, at the bloody battle of Gettysburg. She had one daughter, Marion, a beautiful young lady of seventeen. Marion and Jack thought the world of each other and were all but inseparable.

The sudden taking-off of the colonel had proved a great shock both to the children and to Mrs. Ruthven, and for a long time the lady of the house had lain on a bed of sickness, in consequence.

She was now around, but still weak and pale. Her one consolation was the children, and she clung to them closer than ever.

On several occasions Jack had spoken of enlisting as a drummer boy, but Mrs. Ruthven would not listen to it.

"No, no, Jack! I cannot spare you!" had been her words. "One gone out of the family is enough."

And Marion, too, had clung to him, so that going away became almost an impossibility, although he longed for the glories of a soldier's life, with never a thought of all the hardships and sufferings such a life entails.

The meeting with the Confederate surgeon had filled Jack's head once more with visions of army life, and as he continued to fish he forgot all about the unpleasant encounter, although he remembered that repulsive face well. He was destined to meet the surgeon again, and under most disagreeable circumstances.

"I wish mother would let me join the army," he thought, after hauling in another fish. "I am sure our regiments need all the men they can get. Somehow, we seem to be getting the worst of the fighting lately. I wonder what would happen if the South should be beaten in this struggle?"

Ten minutes passed, when a merry whistle was heard on the road and another boy appeared, of about Jack's age.

"Hullo, Darcy!" cried Jack. "Come to help me fish?"

"I didn't know you were fishing," answered Darcy Gilbert, a youth who lived on the plantation next to Jack. "Are you having good luck?"

"First-rate. I was getting ready to go home, but now you have come I'll stay a while longer."

"Do, Jack; I hate to fish alone. But I say, Jack—" And then Darcy broke off short.

"What were you going to say?"

"Oh, nothing!"

There was a minute of silence, during which Darcy baited his hook and threw it in.

"You look as if you had something on your mind. Darcy," went on Jack, after his friend had brought in a fine haul apparently without appreciating the sport. "Did you meet a Confederate surgeon on the road?"

"No, I came across the plantation. What of him?"

"He came this way, and we got into a regular row because I wouldn't clear right out and give him the whole of the bridge."

"He didn't hit you, did he?"

"Not much! If he had I would have pitched into him, I can tell you, big as he was!" And Jack's eyes flashed in a way that proved he meant what he said.

"No, I didn't meet him, but I met St. John Ruthven, your cousin. Jack, do you know that that young man is a regular bully, even if he is a dandy?"

"Yes, I know it, Darcy."

"And he is down on you."

"I know that too. But why he dislikes me I don't know, excepting that I don't like to see him paying his addresses to my sister Marion. Marion is too good for such a man."

"Is he paying his addresses to her?"

"Well, he is with her every chance he can get."

"Does Marion like him?"

"Oh! I reckon she does in a way. He is always so nice to her—much nicer than he has ever been to me."

"Has he ever spoken to you about yourself?" went on Darcy Gilbert, with a peculiar look at Jack.

"Oh, yes! often."

"I mean about—well, about your past?" went on Darcy, with some confusion.

"My past, Darcy? What is wrong about my past?"

"Nothing, I hope. But I didn't like what St. John Ruthven said about you."

"But what did he say?"

"I don't know as I ought to tell you. I didn't believe him."

"But I want to know what he did say?" demanded Jack, throwing down his fishing pole and coming up close to his friend.

"Well, if you must know, Jack, he said you were a nobody, that you didn't belong to the Ruthven family at all, and that you would have to go away some day," was the answer, which filled Jack with consternation.

CHAPTER II.

DARCY GILBERT'S STORY.

"He said I didn't belong to the Ruthven family?" said Jack slowly, when he felt able to speak.

"He did, and I told him I didn't believe him."

"But—but—I don't understand you, Darcy. Am I not Jack Ruthven, the son of the late Colonel Martin Ruthven?"

"He says not."

"What! Does he mean to say that my mother isn't my mother at all?" ejaculated Jack, with wide-open eyes.

"That's it exactly, and he added that Marion wasn't your sister."

"I'll—I'll punch his head for that!" was the quick return.

"I felt like doing that, too, Jack, even though he is so much older than either of us. I told him he was a mean fellow and that I wouldn't believe him under oath."

"But how did it all come about?"

"Oh, it started at the boathouse back of Old Ben's place. He wanted to bully me, and I told him I wouldn't let him lord it over me any more than you let him bully you. That got him started, for it seems he was sore over the fact that you took Marion out for a boatride one afternoon when he wanted her to go along with him on horseback. One word brought on another, and at last he said he reckoned you would have to clear out some day—that you were only a low upstart anyway, with no real claim on the Ruthvens."

"He said that, did he?" Jack drew a long breath and set his teeth hard. "Did he try to prove his words?"

"I didn't give him a chance. I was so upset I merely told him I didn't believe him, and came away."

"And where did he go?"

"He started off toward town."

"When he comes back I'm going to find out the truth of this matter."

"I don't believe his story, Jack, and I wouldn't worry myself about it."

"But supposing it were true, Darcy—that I was a—a—nobody, as he says?"

"I should think just as much of you," answered the other lad quickly.

"Thank you for that."

"St. John always talks too much—don't mind him."

"But I shall. If he tells the truth I want to know it—and, if not, I shall take steps to make him take back the stories he is circulating."

"It's a wonder he hasn't gone to the war. Why doesn't he enlist, like the rest of the young men in this neighborhood?"

"He says he must stay with his mother. But the real reason is, I think, that he is a coward."

"Perhaps you are right. I remember once, when there was a cry of mad dog in the town, he hid in a warehouse and was almost scared to death."

"Yes, I remember that, and I remember, too, when Big Bill, the slave, ran away and threatened to kill the first white man he met, St. John hid in the mansion and didn't come outside the door for a week."

"Such a coward wouldn't be above circulating falsehoods."

"I wish I knew just where to find him. I would have it out with him in short order," concluded Jack.

The youth was in no humor for further fishing and soon wound up his line and started for home.

As he passed along over the plantation road his thoughts were busy. Could there be any truth in what St. John Ruthven had said? Was he really a nobody, with no claim upon the lady he called mother and the girl he looked upon as his sister? A chill passed down his backbone, and, as he came in sight of the stately old mansion that he called home, he paused to wipe the cold perspiration from his forehead.

"I will go to mother and ask her the truth," he told himself. "I can't wait to find out in any other way." Yet the thought of facing that kind-hearted lady was not a pleasant one. How should he begin to tell her of what was in his mind?

"Is my mother in?" he asked of the maid whom he met in the hallway.

"No, Massah Jack, she dun went to town," was the answer of the colored girl.

"Did she say when she would be back?"

"No, sah."

"Do you know if my sister is around?"

"She dun gone off not five minutes ago, Massah Jack."

"Where to?"

"I heard her say she was gwine down to Ole Ben's boathouse. I 'spect she dun t'ought yo' was dar."

Jack said no more, but giving the colored girl the fish, to take around to the cook, he ran upstairs, washed and brushed up, and sallied forth to find Marion.

The boathouse which had been mentioned was an old affair, standing upon the shore of a wide bay overlooking the Atlantic ocean. It belonged to a colored man called "Old Ben," a fellow who had once been a slave on the Ruthven plantation.

As Jack approached it he saw Marion sitting on a bench in the shade, with a book in her lap. Instead of reading, however, the girl was gazing out to sea in a meditative way.

"Marion, I was looking for you."

"Oh, Jack! is that you? I thought you had gone fishing for the day."

"I just got home, after catching a pretty good mess. Want to go rowing with me?"

"Yes, I'd like that very much. I was wishing you or Old Ben would come."

"Or, perhaps, St. John?" said Jack inquiringly.

"No; I didn't wish for him, you tease."

"I am glad of it, Marion. I don't want you to give me up for St. John."

"I do not intend to, Jack. But why are you looking so serious. Have you anything on your mind? I never saw you look so thoughtful before."

"Yes, I have a lot on my mind, Marion. Come, I'll tell you when we are out on the bay."

A rowboat was handy and oars were in the rack in the boathouse, and soon the pair were out on the water. Although but a boy, Jack took to the water naturally and handled the oars as skillfully as the average sailor.

When they were about halfway across the bay he ceased rowing and looked earnestly at the girl before him.

"Marion, I want to find out—that is, I've got some questions to ask," he blurted out. "I don't know how to go at it."

"Why, what in the world is the matter, Jack? You were red a moment ago. Now you are as pale as a sheet."

"I want to know about something awfully important."

"I'm sure I cannot imagine what it is."

"Marion, aren't we real sister and brother?"

The question was out at last, and as he asked it his eyes dropped, for he had not the courage to look into her face. He felt her start and give a shiver.

"Oh, Jack! what put that in your head," she said slowly.

"Never mind that. Tell me, are we real sister and brother or not?"

"Jack, we are not."

"Oh, Marion!" The words almost choked him, and for the moment he could say no more.

"We are not real sister and brother, Jack, but to me you will always be as a real brother," and Marion caught his hand and held it tightly.

"And—and mother isn't my—my real mother?" he faltered.

"No, Jack; she is only your foster mother. But she thinks just as much of you as if you were her real son. She has told me that over and over again."

"You are sure of this?"

"Yes, Jack."

"Sure I am a—a nobody." His voice sunk to a mere whisper.

"Yon are not a nobody, Jack. When you were a mere boy of three or four my father and mother adopted you, and you are now John Ruthven, my own brother," and she gave his brown hand another tight squeeze.

He was too confused and bewildered to answer at once. The dreadful news was true, he was not really a Ruthven. He was a nobody—no, he must be *somebody*. But who was he?

CHAPTER III.

A MYSTERY OF THE PAST.

"I do not know that I have done just right by telling you this," went on Marion. "Mother may not approve of it."

"I am glad you told me. I was bound to find out about it, sooner or later."

"That is true, Jack. But both mother and I dreaded that time. We were afraid you might turn from us. And we both love you so much!"

"It is kind of you to say that, Marion." Jack's face flushed. "You couldn't be nicer if you were my real sister."

"And mother loves you so much."

"I know that, too—otherwise she wouldn't have taken me in as she did."

"What put it in your head to ask me this to-day?"

"Something St. John Ruthven said to Darcy Gilbert. St. John said I was an upstart, a nobody."

"St. John had better mind his own business! It was not cousinly for him to interfere!" And Marion's face flushed.

"I suppose he doesn't look at me in the light of a cousin. He considers me an intruder."

"Well, if he won't count you a cousin he need not count me one either—so there!"

"But you must not hurt yourself by standing up for me," cried Jack hastily.

"I will not hurt myself—in the eyes of those whose respect is worth considering. In the eyes of the law you are my real brother, for my parents adopted you. St. John must not forget that."

"But tell me of the past, Marion. Where did I come from, and how did I get here?"

"It's a long story, Jack. Do you see yonder wreck, on Hemlock Bluff rocks?"

"To be sure I do."

"Well, when that wreck came ashore, between ten and eleven years ago, you had been one of the passengers on the boat."

"Me!"

"Yes. I have heard mother tell of it several times. It was a fearful night and Old Ben, he was our slave then, was out on the bluff watching. Presently there was the booming of a signal gun—showing the ship was in distress—and soon the ship came in sight, rocking to and fro, with the wild waves running over her deck. Not a soul was left on board, captain and crew having all gone down in the ocean beyond."

"But where did they find me?"

"On the beach. Old Ben heard a cry of pain and ran in the direction of the sound. Soon he made out the form of a woman, your mother. She had been hurt by being hit with some wreckage. You were in her arms, and as Old Ben came up you cried out: 'Jack is hungry. Give Jack some bread and butter, please.'"

"Yes, yes! I remember something of a storm and of the awful waves. But it's all dreamy-like."

"You were only three or four years old, and the exposure nearly cost you your life. Old Ben took you and your mother to the boathouse and then ran up to the plantation for help. Father went back with him, along with half a dozen men, and they brought you and your mother to the house. I remember that time well, for I was nearly seven years old."

"But my mother, what of her?" asked Jack impatiently.

"Poor dear! she died two days later. The physicians did all they could for her, but the shock had been too great, and she passed away without recovering consciousness."

"Then she told nothing about me—who I was?"

"No. All she did say while she lived was 'Save my husband! Save my darling little Jack.'"

"Then my father must have been on the boat with her?"

"Yes."

"And they did not find his body?"

"No, the only bodies recovered were those of sailors."

"Didn't they try to find out who I was?"

"To be sure, but, although father did his best, he could learn nothing. Your father and mother had taken passage on the ship at the last moment and their names did not appear on the list at the shipping offices, and none of the books belonging to the ship itself were ever recovered."

"Perhaps they are on the wreck!" cried Jack, struck by a sudden idea.

"No, the wreck was searched from end to end, and all of value taken away."

"I'd like to row over and look around."

"You may do so, Jack. I presume the wreck will have more of an interest than ever for you now."

The distance to Hemlock Bluff rocks was a good mile, but Jack soon covered it and, bringing the boat to a safe corner, he assisted Marion out and then leaped out himself.

"This news is enough to make a fellow's head whirl," he observed, as they walked in the direction of the wreck, which lay high up on the beach.

"I suppose that is true, Jack. But do not let it worry you. You are as dear to mother and me as if you were one of the family."

"But I would like to know who I really am."

"Perhaps time will solve the mystery."

Soon the pair were at the wreck, which lay with its bow well up on the rocks and its stern projecting over the sea.

It was no mean task to reach the deck of the wreck, but Jack was a good climber and soon he was aboard. Then he gave Marion a hand up.

The deck of the wreck was much decayed, and they had to be careful how they moved around.

"I am going below," said the youth, after a general look around.

"Be careful. Jack, or you may break a limb," cautioned Marion.

"I don't suppose you care to go down with me?"

"I think not—at least, I will wait until you have been down."

Soon Jack was crawling down the rotted companion way. At the bottom all was dirty and dark. He pushed open the door, which hung upon one rusty hinge, and peered into the cabin.

"I wish I had brought a lantern along," he murmured, as he stepped into the compartment.

As Marion had said, the wreck had been cleared of everything of value. All the furniture was gone and the pantries and state-rooms were bare. From the cabin he passed into several of the staterooms.

"What have you found?" called Marion.

"Nothing much."

"Any mice down there, or spiders?"

"None, so far as I can see."

"Then I'll come down."

Soon Marion was beside Jack, and the pair made a tour of the wreck from bow to stern. Their investigations proved to be highly interesting, and they spent more time below than they had anticipated doing.

"We must get back, Jack," said the girl at last.

"Oh, there is no hurry! Mother is not at home," answered Jack. It seemed a bit odd to call Mrs. Ruthven mother now that he knew she was not his relative.

So fully another hour was spent below, moving from one part of the big wreck to another. Presently Jack came to a sudden stop and listened.

"What a queer noise, Marion!"

"It is the wind rising. We had better be getting back, before the bay grows too rough for rowing."

"You are right."

Jack ran up the companion way and Marion after him. To their surprise the sky was overcast, and the wind was whipping the surface of the bay into numerous whitecaps.

"We must lose no time in getting back!" cried Jack. "As it is, the wind will be dead against us!"

As quickly as possible he assisted Marion over the side, and then both set off on a run for the little cove where the rowboat had been left tied up.

As they gained the boat Jack gave an exclamation of dismay.

"The oars—they are gone!"

He was right. Marion had shifted their position before leaving the craft, and bumping against the rocks had sent them adrift.

CHAPTER IV.

ON BOARD THE WRECK.

"Jack, what shall we do now?" asked Marion, as with a blanched face she gazed into the empty boat.

"Wait—the oars may be close at hand," he replied. "I will make a search."

"And so will I. Oh, we must find them!"

They ran up and down the rocky shore, looking far and near for the oars, but without success. Presently they came to a halt, out of breath with running.

"Gone, sure enough!" groaned the boy. "What a pickle we are in now!"

"We can't stay here, Jack."

"We'll have to stay here, Marion, unless I can find the oars or make substitutes."

"How are you going to make substitutes?"

"I might take some planks from the wreck."

"But you have no tools."

"I have a stout jack-knife."

"It will take a long time, and see, it is already beginning to rain."

Marion was right, the rain had started, and as it grew heavier they withdrew to the shelter of the wreck.

"I wouldn't mind staying here until the shower was over, only I wouldn't want mother to worry about us," went on Marion, when they were safe under cover.

"That's just it. But we do not know if she is home yet."

The rain soon increased, while the thunder rolled in the distance. But they felt fairly safe in the cabin of the wreck, and sat down on a bench running along one of the walls.

"This looks as if it was going to keep up all night," observed Jack, an hour later, after another look at the sky from the top of the companion way.

"Oh, you don't mean we'll have to remain here all night!" exclaimed Marion.

"Perhaps, Marion."

"But I do not wish to remain in such a place all night."

"Are you afraid of ghosts?" and Jack gave a short laugh.

"No, Jack; but you'll admit it isn't a very nice place."

"I know that. But that isn't the worst of it."

"Not the worst of it?"

"No. You must remember that we have nothing to eat or to drink here."

"That is true, but I do not feel much like eating or drinking just now."

"Yes, but you'll be hungry and thirsty before morning, Marion."

"Perhaps. We can drink rain water, if we wish."

Another hour passed and the storm grew more violent. The lightning flashed across the sky and lit up the wreck from end to end. Then a blackness as of night followed.

"We could not row ashore now, even if we had oars," observed Marion, as she listened to the howling of the wind.

"You are right, Marion. My, how it does blow!"

Suddenly, the sounds of footsteps on the deck of the wreck reached their ears.

"Somebody is coming!" said Jack, and looked up the companion way. "Why, it's Old Ben!"

He was right; it was Ben the fisherman who had put in an appearance, market basket in hand.

"Marion! Jack! Am dat yo'?" came in an anxious voice.

"Yes, Ben!" cried both.

"What brought you?" continued the boy.

"I dun thought yo' was a-wantin' ob Ole Ben," grinned the colored man. "I seed yo' rowin' off an' I didn't see yo' cum back, so I says to myself, 'Da is stuck fast on de wreck.' An' den I says, 'Da aint got nuffin to eat.' So ober I comes, an' wid a basketful of good t'ings from de plantation." And he held up the market basket. He was soaked from the rain, and the water ran from his clothing in a stream.

"Ben, you are a jewel!" burst out Marion and patted his wet coat-sleeve affectionately.

At this the old negro grinned broadly. He had always been a privileged character on the Ruthven plantation, and being set free had not ended his affection for his former mistress and her children.

"It was very kind to come over," said Jack. "Does mother know we are here?"

"I dun left word dat I was comin' ober an' dat I thought yo' was yeah, sah," answered Ben.

He had brought all the good things necessary, along with plates, cups, knives and forks, and soon had the spread ready for them. Then he went off to another part of the wreck to wring out his wet garments.

"It was very nice of Old Ben to come to us," said Marion, while eating. "It must have been no easy matter to row from the shore to the rocks."

"Ben is as good a boatman as there is in these parts, Marion. It was kind, and he ought to be rewarded for it."

"Mamma will reward him, beyond a doubt."

The storm kept increasing in violence, and before the strange meal was disposed of the thunder and lightning were almost incessant. Ben had brought a candle along—knowing the darkness inside of the wreck—and this was all the light they possessed, outside of what Nature afforded.

Ben was just putting the dishes back into the basket when there came an extra heavy flash of lightning, followed immediately by a rending clap of thunder which almost paralyzed Marion and Jack. There was a strange smell in the air, and both found their blood tingling in a manner that was new to them.

"The wreck—it's been struck by lightning!" gasped Jack, when he could speak.

"Dat's a fac'!" came from Old Ben. "It was jess like de crack ob doom, wasn't it?"

He ran on deck, and Jack followed him, with Marion on the bottom of the companion way, not knowing whether to go up or remain below.

The bolt had struck the wreck near the stern, ripping off a large part of the woodwork, and had passed along to one side. Just below the deck line a lively fire was starting up.

"De wrack am gwine to be burnt up at las'!" ejaculated Old Ben. "We has got to git out, Massah Jack!"

"Come, Marion!" called back the boy. "It's too bad we've got to go out in the rain, but I reckon we can be thankful that our lives have been spared."

"Yes, we can be thankful," answered the girl. "Oh, what a dreadful crack that was! I do not believe I shall ever forget it."

She came on deck all in a tremble, and with the others hurried to the bow of the wreck. It was much easier to climb down than to climb up, and soon all three stood upon the rocks below, where the driving rain pelted them mercilessly.

"I t'ink I can find yo' a bettah place dan dis to stay," said Old Ben. "Come down to de shoah," and he led the way to where he had left his boat. With Jack's assistance the craft was hauled out of the water and turned upside down between two large rocks, and then the three crawled under the temporary shelter.

Thus the night passed, and by morning the storm cleared away. Looking toward the wreck they saw that only a small portion of the upper deck had been burned away, the rain having put the fire out before it gained great headway.

It did not take Old Ben and Jack long to launch the former's craft again, and this done, they all entered and the fisherman started to row them to the mainland. Jack's boat was taken in tow.

"That was certainly quite an adventure," observed Jack, as they landed. "Marion, I reckon you don't want another such."

"No, indeed!" replied the girl, with a shiver. "I don't believe I'll ever go over to the old wreck again."

"It's a wondah dat wreck aint busted up long ago," put in Old Ben.

"It's a wonder the poor people around here haven't carried off the wreckage for firewood, Ben," said Jack.

"Da is afraid to do dat, Massah Jack—afraid some ob de sailors wot was drowned might haunt 'em."

"I see. Well, I don't think the wreck will last much longer," and with these words Jack turned away to follow Marion to the plantation mansion, to interview his foster mother concerning the particulars of the past. Little did the lad dream of what an important part that old wreck was to play in his future life.

CHAPTER V.

OLD BEN HAS A VISITOR.

St. John Ruthven was a young man of twenty-five, tall, thin, and with a face that was a mixture of craftiness and cowardice. He was the son of a half-brother to the late Colonel Ruthven and could boast of but few of the good traits of Marion's family. He lived on a plantation half a mile from the bay and spent most of his time in attention to his personal appearance and in horseback riding, of which, like many other Southerners, he was passionately fond.

It was commonly supposed that St. John Ruthven was rich, but this was not true. His father had left him a good plantation and some money in the bank, but the young planter was a spendthrift and his mother, who doted on her son, was little better, and soon nearly every dollar which had been left by the husband and father had slipped through their fingers. More than this, St. John took but little interest in the plantation, which gradually ran down until it became almost worthless.

"St. John, my dear, we must do something," the mother would say, in her helpless way. "We cannot live like this forever."

"What shall I do?" would be the son's reply. "The plantation isn't worth working and I have no money with which to buy another place. The niggers are getting so they are not worth their keep."

"But you told me yesterday that we had less than a thousand dollars left in the bank."

"It's true, too."

"What do you propose doing when that is gone?"

"Oh! our credit is still good," was the lofty answer.

"But that won't last forever, St. John."

"Something may turn up."

"Everything seems to prosper at Alice's place," went on Mrs. Mary Ruthven, referring to the home of Marion and Jack.

"I know that."

"And we are continually running behind. St. John, you ought to get after the niggers and other help."

"I wasn't cut out for work, mother," was the sour answer.

"But we really must do something," was the half-desperate response.

"I've got an idea in my head, mother. If it works, we'll be all right."

"What is the idea?"

"I think a good deal of Marion. Why shouldn't we marry and join the two plantations? That would give us both a good living."

"I have thought of such a plan myself, St. John. But there may be an objection."

"Do you think Marion would refuse me?"

"She might. In some respects Alice's daughter is rather peculiar."

"But I don't see why she should refuse me. Am I not her equal in social position?"

"What a question! Of course you are. Still she may have her eyes set upon somebody else."

"I know of nobody. Marion is still young."

"Have you sounded her on the subject?"

"Not yet, but I will soon. She has Jack around so much I never get half a chance to talk to her."

"Always that boy! When I visited Alice last I declare she talked of that nobody the whole time,—what a wonderful man she hoped he would make,—and all that. Just as if he was her own flesh and blood!" and Mrs. Mary Ruthven tossed her head disdainfully.

"She was foolish to allow that nobody to think himself a Ruthven. But I have put a spoke into his wheel, I reckon."

"What do you mean? Did you tell Jack the truth?"

"Not exactly. But I gave a pretty broad hint to his intimate friend Darcy Gilbert, and Darcy, of course, will carry the news straight to Jack."

"Oh, St. John! that may cause trouble. Your aunt wished to keep the truth from the boy as long as possible. She told me she did not wish to hurt his feelings."

"He had to learn the truth sooner or later. Besides, I didn't want him to think himself a Ruthven and the equal of Marion and myself," went on St. John loftily.

There was a moment of silence and Mrs. Mary Ruthven gave a long sigh.

"Well, I would not delay speaking to Marion too long," she observed. "Something must be done, that's sure, and if you wait, Marion and her mother may find out how hard up we really are, and then Marion may refuse you on that account."

"I shall see her before long," answered the son.

He had his mind bent on a horseback ride, and was soon in the saddle and off on a road leading along the shore of the bay. He hoped to find Marion in the vicinity of the old boathouse, but when he arrived there nobody was in sight but Old Ben, who was mending one of his fishing nets.

"Ha, Ben! are you alone?" he said, as he dismounted and came into the boathouse.

"Yes, Massah St. John, I'm alone unless there's some ghostes hidin' around yeah!" and the old negro smiled broadly. He understood St. John's character pretty thoroughly and despised him accordingly.

"I thought Marion might be around here."

"She aint been yeah to-day, sah. She an' Jack was out on de bay in dat awful storm yesterday and I reckon it was most too much fo' dem."

"Out in that awful storm! It's a wonder the boat didn't upset."

"Da was ober to de wrack when de big blow came."

"Did they stay there?"

"I went ober after 'em an' da come in dis mornin', Massah St. John."

"Humph! I am surprised that my aunt should trust Marion with that boy."

"Why not, Massah St. John? Jack can manage a boat as well as I can."

St. John tossed his head and flung himself down upon a seat. "I think my aunt makes a fool of herself about that boy. Who is he, anyway? He's only an ocean waif; of low birth, very probably."

"Dat he isn't!" said Old Ben indignantly. "He's a young gen'man, Jack is, an' so was his father."

"Bah! what do you know about his father?"

"He couldn't be Jack's father without bein' a gen'man—dat's wot I know," went on Ben stoutly. "Why, look at de deah chile! How noble an'—an'—handsome he is!"

"Oh, pshaw, Ben! you had better stick to your nets. What do you know about a gentleman?"

"I knows one when I sees one, Massah St. John," was the somewhat suggestive response.

"Oh, do you? And I know an impudent nigger when I see one!" cried St. John angrily.

"No offense, Massah St. John."

"Then be a little more careful of what you say." St. John tugged at the ends of his stubby mustache. "I wish I had that boy under my care," he went on.

"S'posin' you had, sah?"

"I'd teach him his place. Why should he be reared as a gentleman—he, a poor waif of the sea? Probably he is the son of some low mechanic, perhaps of a Northern mudsill, and my aunt—think of it, my aunt—must bring him up as a Southern gentleman!" The young man leaped up and began to pace the boathouse floor nervously. "I suppose she'll leave him a large legacy in her will."

"I 'spect you is right, Massah St. John; dat boy will be pervided for, suah as my name's Ben."

"You talk as if you already knew something of this?" said St. John quickly.

"I does know somet'ing, sah."

"Has my aunt ever spoken to you on the subject, Ben?"

"I don't know as I ought to answer dat dar question, Massah St. John."

"Then she has spoken. What did she say?"

The colored man hesitated.

"As I said befo', sah, I don't rackon I ought to answer dat dar question."

"But you must answer me, Ben—to keep silent is foolish. Rest assured I have the best interests of my aunt and Marion at heart. Now what did she say?"

"Well, sah, if yo' must know, she said as how she was gwine to leave Massah Jack half de prop'ty."

St. John leaped back in amazement.

"You don't mean that, Ben!" he gasped.

"Yes, sah, I does mean it."

"Half the property?"

"Yes, sah."

"He doesn't deserve it!"

At this the old negro shrugged his huge shoulders.

"Rackon de missus knows what she wants to do."

"But it is not right—to give the boy half the estate. I suppose the other half will go to Marion."

"Yes, sah."

The young man's face grew pale, and he began to pace the floor again.

"She never mentioned me in connection with this, did she?"

"No, sah."

"And yet I am her nephew."

"Rackon she dun thought yo' was rich enough, Massah St. John."

"Perhaps I am, Ben. But it is strange that my own flesh and blood should forget me, to take up with a nobody. Did my aunt ever speak of the particulars of what she intended to do?"

"No, sah."

"Humph! It's strange. I must look into this." And a few minutes later St. John Ruthven was off on horseback, in a frame of mind far from pleasant.

CHAPTER VI.

MRS. RUTHVEN'S STORY.

"I am so glad to see you both back, safe and sound!"

It was Mrs. Alice Ruthven who spoke, as she embraced first her daughter and then Jack.

"And we are glad enough to get back, mother," answered Marion.

"I was so frightened, even after Old Ben went after you. We watched the lightning, and when it struck the wreck—" Mrs. Ruthven stopped speaking and gave a shiver.

"We weren't in such very great danger," answered Jack. Then he looked at the lady curiously.

"What is it, Jack? You have something on your mind," she said quickly.

The youth looked at Marian, who turned red.

"I—I—that is, mother, Jack knows the truth," faltered the girl.

"The truth?" repeated Mrs. Ruthven slowly.

"Yes, Marion has told me the truth," said Jack, in as steady a voice as he could command. "And so I—I—am not your son." He could scarcely speak the words.

"Oh, Jack!" The lady caught him in her arms. "So you know the truth at last?" She kissed him. "But you are my son, just as if you were my own flesh and blood. You are not angry at me for keeping this a secret so long? I did it because I did not wish to hurt your feelings."

"No, I am not angry at you, Mrs. Ruth—"

"Call me mother, Jack."

"I am not angry, mother. You have been very kind to me. But it is so strange! I can't understand it all," and he heaved a deep sigh.

"You have been a son to me in the past, Jack; I wish you to continue to be one."

"But I have no real claim upon you."

"Yes, you have, for my late husband and myself adopted you."

"Marion told me that you never heard one word regarding my past."

"She told the truth. We tried our best, but every effort ended in failure. Your mother called you Jack ere she died, and that was all."

"What of our clothing? Was none of it marked, or had she nothing in her pocket?"

"No, the clothing was not marked, and she had nothing in her pocket but a lace handkerchief, also unmarked. That handkerchief I have kept, with the clothing. And I have also kept a ring she wore upon one of her fingers."

"Was that marked?"

"It had been, but it was so worn that we could not make out the marking, nor could the two jewelers by whom we had the ring inspected."

"I would like to see the ring."

"I will get it," returned Mrs. Ruthven, and left the room. Soon she came back with a small jewel casket, from which she took a ring and a very dainty lace handkerchief.

"Here is the ring," she said, as she passed it over to Jack.

"It looks like a wedding ring," said the youth, as he gazed at the circlet of gold.

"I believe it is a wedding ring."

Jack looked inside and saw some markings, but all were so faint that it was impossible to make out more than the figures 1 and 8.

"Those figures stand for eighteen hundred and something, I imagine," said Mrs. Ruthven. "They must give the year when your mother was married."

"I suppose you are right."

"The ring belongs to you, Jack. I would advise you to be careful of it."

"If you please, I would like to have you keep it for the present."

"I will do that willingly."

The handkerchief was next examined. But it seemed to be without markings of any kind, and was soon returned to the jewel case along with the ring.

"Now tell me how Marion came to tell you of the past," said Mrs. Ruthven, after putting the jewel case away.

"I made her tell me the truth," said Jack.

"But how did you suspect this at first?"

"Because of something St. John said to Darcy Gilbert."

"What did he say?"

"Oh, it doesn't matter much—now, mother. He told Darcy I wasn't your son."

"What else did he say?"

"Oh, I think I had better not say."

"But you must tell me, Jack; I insist upon knowing."

"He told Darcy that I was a nobody, and that I would have to go away some day."

At these words Mrs. Ruthven's face flushed angrily.

"St. John is taking too much upon his shoulders," she cried. "This is no business of his."

"I may be a nobody, but, but"—Jack stammered—"if he says anything to me, I am afraid there will be a row."

"He shall not say anything to you. I will speak to him about this. Leave it all to me."

"But he shall not insult me," said Jack sturdily.

Marion had left the apartment, to change her clothing, so she did not hear what was said about St. John. A few words more on the subject passed between the lady of the plantation and the youth, and then the talk shifted back to Jack's past.

"Some day I am going to find out who I am." said the boy. "There must be some way to do this."

"Are you then so anxious to leave me, Jack?" asked Mrs. Ruthven, and the tears sprang into her eyes.

"No, no, mother; I will not leave you so long as you wish me to stay!" he exclaimed. "It isn't that. But this mystery of the past must be solved."

"Well, I will help you all I can. But do not hope for too much, my boy, or you may be disappointed," and then she embraced him again.

Running up to his bedroom, Jack quickly changed the suit which had been soaked the night before for a better one, and then came below again. He hardly knew what to do with himself. The news had set his head in a whirl. At last he decided to go out riding on a pony Mrs. Ruthven had given him a few weeks before.

The pony was soon saddled by one of the stable hands, and Jack set off on a level road running between the two Ruthven plantations. At first he thought to ask Marion to accompany him, but then decided that he was in no humor to have anybody along.

"I must think this out by myself," was the way he reasoned, and set off at a brisk pace under the wide-spreading trees.

He was less than quarter of a mile away from home when he came face to face with St. John, who was returning from his visit to Old Ben's boathouse.

As the two riders approached each other, the young man glared darkly at our hero.

"Hullo, where are you bound?" he demanded sharply.

"I don't think that is any of your business, St. John," replied Jack, who was just then in no humor to be polite.

"Humph! you needn't get on your high horse about it!"

"I am not on a high horse, only on a small pony."

"Don't joke me, Jack—I don't like it."

"As you please, St. John."

"What's got into you this morning?" demanded the young man curiously.

"Well, if you want to know, I don't like the way you have been talking about me."

"Oho! so that is how the wind blows."

"You have taken the pains to call me a nobody," went on Jack hotly.

"I told the truth, didn't I?"

"I consider myself just as good as you, St. John Ruthven."

"Do you indeed!" sneered the spendthrift.

"I do indeed, and in the future I will thank you to be more careful of what you say about me."

"I have a right to tell the truth to anybody I please."

"I don't deny that. But I consider my blood just as good as yours."

"Do you? I don't."

"Your opinion isn't worth anything to me."

"Humph! still riding a high horse, I see. Let me tell you, you are not half as good as a Ruthven, and never will be. How my aunt could take you in is a mystery to me."

"She is not as hard-hearted as you are."

"She is very foolish."

"She is my foster mother, and I'll thank you to speak respectfully of her," cried Jack, his eyes flashing.

"Of course you'll stick by her—as long as she'll let you. You have a nice ax to grind."

"I don't understand your last words."

"She owns considerable property, and you will try to get a big share of it for yourself, when she dies."

"I have never given her property a thought. I want only what is rightfully coming to me."

"There is nothing coming to you by right. The property ought to go to Marion and the other Ruthvens."

"By other Ruthvens I suppose you mean yourself."

"I am one of them."

"Are you so anxious to get hold of my aunt's plantation?"

"I don't want to see my aunt waste it on such a low upstart as you!"

Jack's eyes flashed fire, and riding close to St. John he held up his little riding whip.

"You shan't call me an upstart!" he ejaculated. "Take it back, or I'll hit you with this!"

"You won't dare to touch me!" howled St. John in a rage. "You are an upstart, and worse, to my way of thinking."

Scarcely had the words left his lips when Jack brought down the riding whip across the young man's shoulders and neck, leaving a livid red mark behind.

"Oh!" howled the spendthrift, and gave a jerk backward on the reins, which brought his horse up on his hind legs. "How dare you! I'll—I'll kill you for that!"

"Do you take it back or not?" went on Jack, raising the whip again.

Instead of replying St. John reached over to hit the youth with his own whip. But Jack dodged, and then struck out a second time. The blow landed upon St. John's hand, and he jerked back quickly. The movement scared the horse, and the animal plunged so violently that the rider was thrown from the saddle into some nearby bushes. Then the horse galloped away, leaving St. John to his fate.

CHAPTER VII.

A SETBACK FOR ST. JOHN.

"Now see what you have done!" roared St. John, as soon as he could scramble from the bushes.

His face was scratched in several places and his coat was torn at one elbow.

"It was your fault as much as mine," retorted Jack.

"No such thing. You had no right to pitch into me."

"And you had no right to call me names."

"My horse has run away," stormed the young man.

"So I see."

"If he is lost or hurt you'll be responsible."

"He is running toward home. I reckon he'll be all right."

"What am I to do?"

"That's your lookout."

"Get down and let me ride your pony home."

"I will do no such thing!" cried Jack. The little steed was very dear to him.

"Do you expect me to walk?"

"You can suit yourself about that, St. John. Certainly I shan't carry you," and Jack began to move off.

"Stop! don't leave me like this."

"You are not much hurt. Do you want to continue the fight?"

"I don't calculate to fight a mere boy like you. Some day I'll give you a good dressing down for your impudence."

"All right; when that time comes, I'll be ready for you," returned Jack coolly, and without further words he rode away.

Standing in the middle of the road, St. John Ruthven shook his fist after the youth.

"I hate you!" he muttered fiercely. "And I'll not allow you to come between me and my aunt's property, remember that!" But the words did not reach Jack, nor were they intended for his ears.

There was a spring of water not far away, and going to this St. John washed his face and his hands. Then he combed his hair with a pocket-comb he carried, and brushed his clothing as best he could. He was more hurt mentally than physically, and inwardly boiled to get even with our hero.

Left to himself, he hardly knew what to do. He was satisfied that his horse would go home as Jack had said, but he was in no humor to follow the animal.

"I've a good mind to call on Aunt Alice and tell her what a viper he is," he said to himself. "Perhaps I can get her to think less of him than she does—and that will be something gained."

He walked slowly toward the plantation. When he came within sight of the garden he saw Marion in a summerhouse, arranging a bouquet of flowers which she had just cut.

The sight of his cousin put his heart in a flutter and made him think of the talk he had had with his mother. Why should he not propose to her at once? The sooner the better, to his way of thinking. That Marion might refuse him hardly entered his head. Was he not the best "catch" in that neighborhood?

"How do you do, Marion?" he said, as he strode up to the summerhouse.

"Why, St. John, is that you?" returned the girl. "I did not see you riding up."

"I came on foot," he went on, as he came in and threw himself on a bench. "It's warm, too."

"It is warm. Shall I send for some refreshments?"

"No, don't bother just now, Marion. I came over to see you alone."

"Alone?" she said in some surprise.

"Yes, alone, Marion. I have something very important to say to you."

She did not answer, but turned away to fix the bouquet.

"Can you guess what I wish to say?" he went on awkwardly.

"I haven't the remotest idea, Cousin St. John."

"I want to tell you how much I love you, Cousin Marion."

"Oh!"

"Don't think that I speak from sudden impulse. I have loved you for years, but I wished to wait until you were old enough to listen to me."

"And you think I am old enough now?" she said, with a faint smile. "Mamma thinks me quite a girl still."

"You are old enough to marry, if you wish, Marion."

"Marry?" She laughed outright. "Oh, St. John, don't say that. Why, I don't intend to marry in a long, long time—if at all."

His face fell, and he bit his lip. Certainly this was not the answer he had expected.

"But I want you!" he burst out, still more awkwardly. "I want to—to protect you from—er—from Jack."

"Protect me from Jack?"

"Yes, Marion. You know what he is, a mere nobody."

"Jack is my brother."

"He is not, and you know it."

"He is the same as if he were my brother, St. John."

"Again I say he is not. He is a mere upstart, and he will prove a snake in the grass unless you watch him. Your mother made a big mistake when she adopted him."

"There may be two opinions upon that point."

"He knows your mother is rich. Mark my word, he will do all he can, sooner or later, to get her property away from her."

"I will not believe evil of Jack."

"You evidently think more of him than you do of me!" sneered the spendthrift, seeing that he was making no headway in his suit.

"I do not deny that I think the world and all of Jack. He is my brother in heart, if not in blood—and I will thank you to remember that after this," went on Marion in a decided tone.

"You will learn of your mistake some time—perhaps when it is too late."

"Jack is true to the core, and as brave as he is true. Why, he would go to the war if mamma would give her consent."

At this St. John Ruthven winced.

"Well—er—I would go myself if my mother did not need me at home," he stammered. "She must have somebody to look after the plantation. We can't trust the niggers."

"Many men have gone to the front and allowed their plantations to take care of themselves. They place the honor of their glorious country over everything else."

"Well, my mother will not allow me to go—she has positively forbidden it," insisted St. John, anxious to clear his character.

This statement was untrue; he had never spoken to his mother on the subject, thinking she might urge him to go to the front. His plea that he must look after the plantation was entirely of his own making.

"Supposing we should lose in this struggle—what will become of your plantation then?"

At this St. John grew pale.

"I—I hardly think we will lose," he stammered. "We have plenty of soldiers."

"But not as many as the North has. General Lee could use fifty thousand more men, if he could get them."

"Well, I shall go to the front when I am actually needed, Marion; you can take my word on that. But won't you listen to what I have told you about my feeling for you?"

"No, St. John; I am too young to fall in love with anybody. I shall at least wait until this cruel war is over."

"But I can hope?"

She shook her head. Then she picked up her bouquet.

"Will you come up to the house with me?"

"Not now, Marion. Give my respects to my aunt and tell her I will call in a day or two again. And, by the way, Marion, don't let her think hard of me because of Jack. I desire only to see to it that the boy does not do you mischief."

"As I said before, I will listen to nothing against dear Jack, so there!" cried Marion, and stamping her foot, she hurried toward the house.

St. John Ruthven watched her out of sight, then turned and stalked off toward the roadway leading to his home.

"She evidently does not love me as I thought," he muttered to himself. "And I made a mess of it by speaking ill of Jack. Confound the luck! What had I best do now? I wish I could get that boy out of the way altogether, I really do."

CHAPTER VIII.

THE HOME GUARDS OF OLDVILLE.

The week to follow the events recorded in the last chapter was a trying one for the inhabitants of Oldville, as the district around the Ruthvens' plantation was called.

The army of the North had pressed the army of the South back steadily day after day, until the Confederates were encamped less than four miles away from Jack's home. For two days the cannon-firing could be distinctly heard, and the women folks were filled with dread, thinking the invaders from the North were about to swoop down upon their homes and pillage them.

"Oh, Jack! do you think they will come here?" was the question Marion asked at least a dozen times.

"They had better not," was the sturdy reply. "If they do, they will find that even a boy can fight."

"But you could do nothing against an army, Jack."

"Perhaps not. But I'll do what I can to protect you and mother."

"Old Ben told me that you and Darcy Gilbert were organizing a Home Guard."

"Yes; we have organized a company of boys. We have twenty-three members, and I am the captain," answered Jack, with just a bit of pride in his tones.

"Then you are Captain Jack!" exclaimed Marion. "Let me congratulate you, captain. But have you any weapons?"

"Yes. I have an old sword and also a pistol, and all of the others have pistols or guns. I think, if we were put to it, we might do our enemy some damage."

"No doubt, since I know you and Darcy can shoot pretty straight. You ought to ask St. John to join the command."

"Not much, Marion! Don't you know that St. John is a coward at heart, even if he is a man?"

"Yes, I know it. One of the colored help on his plantation told Old Ben that the cannon-firing so close at hand made him so uneasy he couldn't eat or sleep."

"Is it possible! Now the cannon-firing simply makes me crazy to be at the front, to see what is going on, and to take part."

"Then you must be a born soldier, Jack." Marion heaved a sigh. "Oh, I wish this war was over! Why must the men of the South and the North kill each other?"

"The world has always had wars and always will, I reckon. Do you want to come to town and see us drill?"

"Will it be safe?"

"I think so, Marion. I don't believe the enemy are coming here very soon."

Soon after this Jack and Marion were on their way to Oldville, a sleepy town containing two general stores, a tavern, and a blacksmith shop.

In front of the tavern was a large green, and here a number of boys were playing various games.

"Hurrah, here comes Captain Jack!" was the cry, when our hero appeared.

"Are we to drill to-day?" questioned Darcy Gilbert, as he ran up and nodded to Marion.

"If you will," said Jack. His new honors had not made him in the least dictatorial.

"All right," returned Darcy.

He was first lieutenant of the company, which had styled itself the Oldville Home Guard, and he quickly summoned the young soldiers together.

All had uniforms, made of regular home suits with stripes of white sewed down the trouser-legs and around the coat-sleeves. The boys with pistols were placed in the front rank, those with guns in the second rank. One lad had a drum and another a fife.

"Company, attention!" ordered Jack, coming to the front with drawn sword, and the boys drew up in straight rows across the green. The drum rattled, and presently quite a crowd of old men, women, and children collected to see the drill.

"Carry—arms!" went on Jack, and the guns came to a carry, and likewise the pistols. "Present—arms! Shoulder—arms! Forward—march!"

"Dum! dum! dum, dum, dum!" went the drummer, and off marched the company to the end of the green.

"Right—wheel!" came the next command, and the boys wheeled with the order of a veteran body, for each was enthusiastic to do his best. "Forward!" and they marched on again, and so the marching kept up until the square had been covered several times.

"Halt!" Thus the commanding went on. "Load! Take aim! Fire!"

And twenty-odd gun and pistol hammers came down with a sharp clicking, for none of the weapons were loaded, the boys saving their powder and ball until such time as they might actually be needed. A short parade around the main streets followed, and then Jack dismissed the company.

"It was splendid!" cried Marion enthusiastically. "I declare, Jack, how did you ever get them drilled so nicely?"

"Oh! the fellows take to it naturally. Besides, Darcy did as much as I did."

"No, Jack is our chief drillmaster," put in Darcy. "He takes to soldiering as a duck takes to a pond."

"It's wonderful. Still, I hope you never have to go to war," concluded Marion.

"If we do, we'll try to give a good account of ourselves," said Darcy, as Marion walked away.

"Indeed we will!" cried our hero.

Now she was in town Marion concluded to do some shopping, and accordingly made her way to one of the general stores, a place kept by Lemuel Blackwood, one of the oldest merchants in that part of the State.

Blackwood's store was usually crowded with goods of every description, but the war had all but wrecked his trade, and his stock was scanty and shop-worn.

"How do you do, Marion?" said he, when the girl entered. He had known her from childhood.

"How do you do, Mr. Blackwood?" she returned.

"Pretty fairly, for an old man, Marion. That is, so far as my health goes. Business is very poor, though."

"The war has taken the people's money."

"Yes, yes! It is awful! Sometimes I think it will never end."

"Do you think we will win, Mr. Blackwood?"

At this the old man shook his head slowly.

"I used to hope so, Marion. But now—the most of our best soldiers have been shot down. The North can get new recruits, but we don't seem to have many more men to go to the front."

"Have you any more calico like that which I got a few weeks ago?"

"No, I can't get a single piece, no matter how hard I try."

"What have you in plain dress goods?"

"Nothing but what I showed you before. I tried to get something new last week, but the wholesale houses had nothing, and couldn't say when anything new would come in. Their business has been wrecked, just as mine has been. Two of the best houses I used to do business with are bankrupt."

"Then show me what you have again, please. Mamma and I must have something, even if it is out of date. We'll wear it for the honor of the South."

At this old Mr. Blackwood smiled. "You are a loyal girl, Marion. I like to see it in a person, especially in one who is young. It shows the right training."

"But supposing I was a Northerner," said Marion, with a sly twinkle in her eye.

"It would make no difference in my opinion."

"You believe people should be true to their convictions?"

"Yes, no matter what side they stand upon. We think we are right, and are willing to fight for our opinions. They think they are right, and they are willing to fight, too."

"But who is right?"

Mr. Blackwood shrugged his shoulders. "Let us trust that God will bring this difficulty to a satisfactory conclusion. If we lose in this war, my one hope is that the South will not lose everything—that the North will be generous."

"But they say Grant is a stubborn general. That he will demand everything of General Lee."

"I cannot believe it. I have a cousin who knew Grant, and he said Grant was not so hard-hearted as painted."

"Some say the South, if defeated, will be held in virtual slavery by the North."

"Yes, some hot-heads say everything. I had such a fellow in here yesterday; a surgeon in our army, who gave his name as Dr. Mackey. He was ranting around, declaring that, if we lost, the Northern soldiers would march clear through to New Orleans and loot and burn every village, town, and city, and that neither life nor property would be safe. His talk was enough to scare a timid person most to death."

"A surgeon in our army," said Marion. She had been told by Jack of the meeting on the bridge. "What kind of a looking man was he?"

As well as he could Mr. Blackwood described the individual.

"Did he seem to have a finger on one hand doubled up and stiff?"

"Yes. Do you know him, Marion?"

"I know of him. He met Jack on a bridge some days ago and ordered him off as if Jack were a slave."

"He appeared to be as headstrong as he was unreasonable. I have seen him around here several times, but I cannot make out what he is doing here. He asked me about the wreck on Hemlock Bluff rocks."

"What!" and Marion showed her surprise.

"Yes. He said he had heard of the wreck and was curious to visit it."

"That was strange."

"I asked him why he wished to visit the wreck, but he did not answer the question."

At this point some other customers came in and the conversation was changed. Marion bought what she wanted and went out, and presently joined Jack on the way home.

"It was odd that surgeon should want to visit the wreck," was our hero's comment, after he had heard what the girl had to say. "I wonder if he knows anything of the ship and her passengers? If he does, I would like to interview him, uncivil as he is."

CHAPTER IX.

DR. MACKEY INVESTIGATES.

A few days later Old Ben was just preparing to go out in his boat when a visitor appeared at the boathouse. The man was clad in the faded uniform of a Confederate surgeon, and proved to be Dr. Mackey.

"Good-mornin', sah," said Old Ben politely, as the doctor leaped from the saddle and came forward.

"Good-morning," returned the surgeon shortly. "Can you supply me with a glass of good drinking water? I left my flask at camp, and I am dry."

"We has de best ob watah heah, sah," returned Old Ben, and proceeded to obtain a goblet. "Does yo' belong to de army?"

"Yes, I am a surgeon attached to the Fifth Virginia regiment." The visitor gazed around him curiously. "Is this your boathouse?"

"Kind o', sah. It belongs to de Ruthven plantation. But when my ole massa—Heaben bless his spirit—sot me free, he gib me de right to use de boathouse so long as I pleased. I lives in yonder cabin on de bluff."

"Ah! then you were one of Mr. Ruthven's slaves?"

"Colonel Ruthven, sah," said the colored man, with emphasis on the military title.

"He is dead?"

"Yes, sah; killed at de bloody battle ob Gettysburg. He was leadin' a charge when a bullet struck him in de head."

"Too bad, truly. Did he leave much of a family?"

"A widow, sah, an' two chillen, a boy an' a girl."

"I see." The doctor drank the water thoughtfully. "Did—er—I mean, I think I have seen the two young people. They don't seem to resemble each other very much."

"Well, you see, da aint persackly brother an' sister."

"No?" and the surgeon raised his heavy eyebrows as if in surprise.

"No, sah. Massah Jack is only de 'dopted son ob de late colonel."

"Ah, is that really so? A—er—nephew, perhaps?"

"No, he aint no kin to de Ruthvens. He was washed ashoah from a wrack ten or 'leben years ago. I wouldn't tell dis, only it has become public property durin' de las' two weeks."

Dr. Mackey started back. "Ha! I have found the boy at last!" he muttered to himself, as he began to walk the floor.

"What did you say, sah?"

"It's quite like a romance, my man. I should like to hear more of the boy's story."

"Dere aint much to tell, massah. It blowed great guns durin' dat storm. De passengers an' crew was washed ashoah from de wrack, but de only ones wot came to de beach alive was Massah Jack an' his poor dear mother."

"And the mother—" The doctor paused.

"She only libed fo' two days. She died up to de house, leabin' de boy to Mrs. Ruthven. De missus promised to look after de boy as her own—an' she has gone dun it, too, sah."

"Then Mrs. Ruthven doesn't know whose son he really is?"

"No, sah. De boy's mammy couldn't tell nuffin, she was so much hurt."

"But what of the boy's father?"

"He was drowned wid de rest ob de passengers."

"Hard luck—for the boy." The surgeon continued to pace the floor.

"By the way, what is your name?" he asked presently.

"Ben, sah."

"There is a dollar for you."

"T'ank yo', massah; you is a real gen'man," and Ben's face relaxed into a broad smile.

"You were going out in your boat, I believe."

"Yes, massah. But if I kin do anyt'ing fo' yo'—"

"What of this wreck? Is it the same that one can see from the bluff?"

"Yes, massah, de werry same."

"It's remarkable that it should survive so long."

"Well, yo' see, sah, de rocks am werry high, so de most ob de storms don't git no chance at de wrack. Dat storm wot put de boat up dar was de mos' powerful dat I eber seen in all my born days."

"Is it possible to board the wreck now?"

"Oh, yes, sah! I was ober dar only a few days ago. De ship was struck by lightning in dat las' storm, but de rain put out de fiah."

"I would like to visit the wreck. I have some time to spare to-day, and I am curious to see how such a big vessel looks when cast up high and dry on the rocks."

"I can take yo' ober, sah."

"Very well; do so, and I'll give you another dollar."

"I'll be ready in a minute, as soon as I gits my fishing tackle an' bait out of de boat, sah."

Ben hurried to his craft. As he was lifting his things out he saw a man strolling near. The individual proved to be St. John Ruthven, who had come in that direction in hope of seeing Marion alone.

"Hullo, Ben!" cried St. John. "See anything of Marion today?"

"She dun went out in a boat, sah."

"With Jack?"

"Yes, sah."

"What, after that experience in the storm?"

"Yes, sah."

"I should think they would be afraid."

"Da aint so afraid as some folks is, Massah St. John."

"Do you mean that as an insult to me, you good-for-nothing nigger?"

"No, sah. I mean Miss Marion an' Massah Jack are wery stout-hearted."

"My aunt is foolish to let Marion go out with that boy. Some day Marion will be drowned."

"Jack knows wot he is doin', I rackon, sah."

"You don't know him. He is thoroughly reckless. I presume as a nobody his life isn't worth much, but—"

"I rackon his life is as sweet to him as yours is to yo', Massah St. John."

"Can you take me out in a boat after them?"

"Sorry, sah, but I'se gwine to take dis gen'man out, sah."

St. John turned and saw Dr. Mackey standing near, the surgeon having come from the boathouse to listen in silence to the conversation which was taking place.

He had met the doctor at the Oldville tavern the evening before, and bowed stiffly.

"I am sorry to disappoint you, Mr. Ruthven," said the doctor; "but I am curious to visit the old wreck on Hemlock Bluff rocks. Perhaps this man has another boat—"

"Oh, it doesn't matter, Dr. Mackey," answered St. John.

"You are evidently a cousin to Miss Marion Ruthven."

"I am."

"And a cousin to the lad named Jack."

"He is no cousin of mine—even though my aunt has foolishly treated him as her son."

"Why foolishly?"

"He is a waif of the sea—cast up from that wreck; yet my aunt presents him to the world as a Ruthven—when he may be of very low birth."

"Evidently you are proud of your name."

"I am proud, sir, for there is no family in South Carolina which bears a better name. We are descended from St. George Ruthven, one of the knights of Queen Elizabeth's reign."

"I congratulate you, sir, and I now understand how this matter grates upon you. But permit me to state, the boy may prove to be of as high birth as yourself."

"What, Jack? Never!"

"Do not say that. Strange things have happened in this world."

"But he looks as if he came of low birth," responded St. John haughtily.

"There I must disagree with you, Mr. Ruthven."

"Dat's de talk!" muttered Old Ben, as he eyed St. John darkly. "Massah Jack's as good as dat coward any day!"

"As you please, doctor; but I shall hold to my opinion."

Dr. Mackey shrugged his shoulders.

"You have that right. Come, Ben, we will be on the way. Mr. Ruthven, allow me to bid you good-day," and the doctor bowed stiffly.

"Good-day," was the curt response.

Soon the surgeon and Old Ben were in the boat, and the negro was rowing swiftly in the direction of the wreck. St. John walked up the shore, but presently turned to view the doctor from a distance.

"He talks as if he knew a thing or two," muttered the spendthrift to himself. "Can it be possible that he knows something of the past, and is going out to the wreck for a purpose?"

CHAPTER X.

THE PAPERS ON THE WRECK.

As the waters of the bay were quiet, it did not take Ben long to row Dr. Mackey over to the wreck on the rocks.

"Be careful how you steps out, sah," said the colored man. "De rocks am slippery, an' you kin twist an ankle widout half tryin', sah."

"I will be careful, Ben. So this is the wreck?"

"Yes, sah."

"I presume all that was movable in the ship has been carried off?"

"Long ago, sah."

"But the inside of the ship itself was not torn out?"

"No, sah. De folks around yeah is too afraid ob ghosteses fo' dat."

"Ah, yes! so I heard—at least, I would suppose so," replied the doctor, in some confusion. "By the way, you need not remain here. I will visit the wreck alone. You can come back in an hour or so."

"Wery well, massah."

"But don't forget to come back. I don't want to be left here all night."

"Don't worry, sah; I'll be back fo' dat dollah, sah," and Ben grinned.

"Oh, yes! I forgot about the dollar. Well, you shall have it when you take me back to shore."

The doctor walked slowly toward the wreck, glancing back several times to see if Old Ben was following him.

The colored man rowed away in a thoughtful mood.

"Somet'ing is on dat man's mind, suah!" he muttered to himself. "He's gwine ter do somet'ing."

With difficulty the surgeon climbed up to the deck of the wreck. A desolate spectacle presented itself. Everything was charred by the fire.

"Truly a nice place to come to," said the man to himself. "Now, supposing this thing turns out a wild-goose chase, after all? Let me see, the stateroom was No. 15. I wonder if I can still locate it?"

With caution he descended the companion way and entered the main cabin of the stranded vessel. Here he drew from his pocket a candle and lit it.

He walked slowly toward the side of the cabin until he reached a stateroom bearing the number 7 upon the door.

"Seven," he murmured. "And the second from this is eleven. That shows the numbers on this side are all odd. The next must be thirteen, and the next fifteen."

He held the candle to the door, but the number plate was gone. Without hesitation he pushed upon the door, which was already partly open. It fell back, exposing the interior of the stateroom, now bare of all things movable, and covered with dust and cobwebs.

"A dirty job this," he murmured, and set the candle down upon a beam running along the side of a wall. He gazed around the stateroom curiously, as if hardly knowing what to do next.

"The little closet was set in the wall at the foot of the bed. Now which was the foot of the bed? I'll try both ends." He did so, tapping on the woodwork with his knuckles. Presently he found a hole where there had once been a small knob.

"The closet, sure enough!" he cried, and his face took on a new interest. "Now where is that door-knob?"

He hunted on the floor, but no knob came to view. But a bent nail was handy, and this he inserted into the hole sideways, and pulled with all his force. There was a slight creak, and a small door came open, revealing a dark closet about a foot square and equally deep.

If the room was dirty the closet was more so, for a crack at the top had let in both dirt and water, and at first he could see nothing but a solid cake of dirt before him. Digging into this, he presently uncovered a heavy tin box, painted black.

"Eureka! the box at last!" he cried, in a tone full of pleasure. "I am the lucky one, after all!"

He brought the tin box forth and brushed it off. There was a little padlock in front, and this was locked. Bringing a bunch of keys from his pocket, he began to try them, one after another. At last he found one to fit, and opened the box.

"The papers at last!" he murmured, and his eyes gleamed with expectation. "Let me see what there is." He turned them over. "The marriage certificate for one, and letters from his father about that property. And other letters from her folks—all here, and just what I wanted." He shoved the documents back into the box. "The fortune is mine!"

Returning to the closet he cleaned it out thoroughly, to learn if it contained anything more of value. But there was nothing more there, and presently he blew out the candle, hid the tin box under his coat, and returned to the deck.

Ben was rowing not far away and saw the doctor wave his hand.

"Is yo' ready, massah?" he called out.

"Yes, Ben."

The colored man said no more, but rowed inshore, and in the meantime the doctor hurried down to meet him.

"Did you find any gold, massah?" asked the colored man, his white teeth gleaming.

"Gold! Why, you foolish nigger, what chance is there of finding gold on a wreck over ten years old? The best thing you can do is to break the boat to pieces and take the wood ashore for fuel."

"But de ghosteses, massah! Besides, Mrs. Ruthven wouldn't let us touch dat wrack nohow."

"On account of the boy, I suppose."

"Yes, massah."

"To tell the truth, my man, I have now as much interest in that ship as has that boy or Mrs. Ruthven. It brings back an exciting passage in my life. My visit to the wreck was made to satisfy me concerning several important questions. I was one of the passengers on that ill-fated ship!"

"Golly, massah, yo' don't really mean dat?" And Old Ben's eyes opened widely.

"Yes, I do. I suspected it before; now I am dead certain of it."

At this declaration Old Ben grew quite excited.

"And did yo' know Massah Jack's fadder, sah?"

"Yes, my man, I knew him very well," and there was a significant smile on the doctor's face as he spoke.

"And was he a gen'man, sah? St. John Ruthven t'inks he was common white trash."

"He was a gentleman of high family—the son of an English nobleman, although born in this country."

"An' Jack's mudder, sah?"

"Was an American lady—a lady belonging to one of the first families of Massachusetts."

"Golly, a Northerner!" and Ben's face became a study.

"Yes."

"Yo' must visit de house, sah, and tell Mrs. Ruthven 'bout dis. She will want to heah de partic'lars wery much, sah."

"Yes, I will visit the Ruthven home," replied the doctor.

"Yo' know de way, sah?"

"I believe I do."

"I can show yo' de way, an' will do it willingly. So you knew

Jack's fadder an' mudder! Golly, but aint dat strange—after all dese yeahs, too! Jack will want to see yo', ob course."

"And I shall want to see Jack," replied the medical man.

"Jack's a fine lad, sah."

"I am glad to hear it." But, as he spoke, the face of Dr. Mackey became a study.

"Yes, sah; aint no bettah boy in all dese parts, sah."

While talking Ben was rowing steadily, and it was not long before the pair reached shore.

Then the boat was made fast, the oars put away, and the doctor and the colored man started for the Ruthven mansion.

CHAPTER XI.

MRS. RUTHVEN SPEAKS HER MIND.

Leaving the shore of the bay, St. John Ruthven walked slowly toward the home of his aunt.

It irritated him greatly to think that his cousin preferred the society of Jack to his own.

"I must speak to Aunt Alice about this," he said to himself. "It is getting worse and worse."

He found his aunt sitting in the garden reading. She looked up in surprise at his approach.

"Aunt Alice, can you spare me a few minutes?" he said, after the usual greeting.

"Surely, St. John. What is it that you wish?"

"I wish to speak to you about Marion."

"About Marion?" Mrs. Ruthven looked somewhat surprised.

"Yes. I saw her out again in a boat with that boy."

"That boy? Do you mean Jack?"

"Yes. I wonder you trust her to his care—after what happened at the wreck."

"Why should I not? Jack understands how to manage a boat. Marion is safe with her brother."

"But he is not her brother," cried St. John.

"Not in blood, perhaps, but in affection. They have been brought up together as children of one family."

"My dear Aunt Alice, do you think you have done wisely in encouraging this intimacy?" he said earnestly.

"What can you mean?" she demanded. "Jack is fourteen years old and Marion is eighteen."

"Of course. But you know nothing of the boy's parentage. He is an unknown waif, cast upon the shore in his infancy, very possibly of a low family."

"No, you are wrong there. Remember, I saw his mother. Everything indicated her to be a lady. The child's clothing was of fine texture. But even if it were otherwise, he has endeared himself to me by his noble qualities. I regard him as a son."

St. John shrugged his shoulders. "You look upon him with the eyes of affection. To me he seems—"

"Well?"

"A commonplace boy,—a mechanic's child, very possibly,—who is quite out of place among the Ruthvens."

At this Mrs. Ruthven grew indignant.

"You are prejudiced!" she cried. "I will not discuss the matter farther with you. I wish no one to speak to me against Jack. He is as dear to me as Marion herself."

The young man drew a deep breath. "I am silenced, Aunt Alice. But I wish to speak to you about Marion. She is no longer a child, but a young lady."

"Yes, she is now eighteen," answered Mrs. Ruthven slowly. "But to me she seems a child still."

"Well—er—at what age did you marry, aunt?"

"At eighteen."

"Then, Aunt Alice, you cannot be surprised if I have thought of Marion as my future wife. I love her warmly and sincerely."

At this abrupt declaration Mrs. Ruthven was considerably surprised.

"Why, St. John, do you wish to marry that child?" she exclaimed.

"Why not? She is eighteen."

"Yes, but I had never thought of her as old enough to be married. Have you spoken to her?"

"Yes," he returned slowly, and with a cloud on his face.

"And what did she say?"

"Nothing—that is, she was taken by surprise and did not wish to discuss the matter at present."

Mrs. Ruthven drew a breath of relief. "She was sensible. Have you any reason to think that she loves you?"

"I think she will soon. I am not conceited, Aunt Alice, but I think I have a good appearance and—I am a Ruthven."

"You are much older than she, St. John."

"I am, but a man of my age is still a young man."

"I should not object if she loved you, but I have never seen any indications of it."

"Will you let her know that you favor my suit?"

At this Mrs. Ruthven shrugged her shoulders.

"But I am not sure that I do," she returned slowly.

"Have you heard anything to my discredit?" he demanded stiffly.

"No, no, St. John; but don't be precipitate. Let the matter rest for the present."

"Well, if you insist upon it, Aunt Alice," he said, his face falling.

"It seems to me best."

"But still, Aunt Alice, if Marion allows her affections to drift in another direction—"

"I do not think she will, for the present. She is more interested in the war than in anything else. Why, if I would allow it, she would go off and offer her services as a nurse."

"Don't let her go, aunt—I beg of you."

Mrs. Ruthven looked at her nephew curiously.

"What makes you so afraid of this war, St. John?"

"Afraid? I am not afraid exactly," he stammered. "I was thinking of dear Marion. It would be horrible for her to put up with the hardships, and such sights!"

"But somebody must bear such sights and sounds. War is war, and our beloved country must be sustained, even in her darkest hour."

He trembled and turned pale, but quickly recovered.

"What you say is true, Aunt Alice. I have wanted to go to the front, but my mother positively refuses her permission. She is in mortal terror that the Yankees will come to our plantation and loot the place in my absence."

"Do you think you can keep them from coming?"

"No, but I can—er—I can perhaps protect my mother."

"If you went off, she could come over here and remain with me."

"She wishes to remain at home. The old place is very dear to her. It would break her heart to have the enemy destroy it."

"I should not wish our place destroyed. Yet the only way to keep the enemy back is to go to the front and fight them."

"Well—I presume you are right, and I shall go some time—when I can win my mother over," said St. John lamely.

He wanted to speak of Marion again, but, on looking across the garden, saw his cousin and Jack approaching. Soon the pair came up and Marion greeted St. John with a slight bow.

"We have been out rowing, mother," said Jack, as he came up and kissed Mrs. Ruthven. "It was lovely on the bay."

"Did you go far?"

"We went over to Hoskin's beach. Marion rowed part of the way."

"I hope you had a nice time," said St. John stiffly, turning to Marion.

"We had a lovely time," answered the girl. "Jack is the best rower around here."

"Humph! Why, he's only a boy!" sneered the spendthrift.

"Yes, I am only a boy, St. John, but I reckon I can row as good as you," replied our hero warmly. He had not forgotten the encounter on the road.

"Do you, indeed?"

"Yes, I do. Some day we can try a race. I'll give you choice of boats and beat you."

At this Marion set up a merry laugh.

"I believe Jack can beat you at rowing, St. John," she said.

"I never race with boys," answered the spendthrift, more stiffly than ever.

"I'll race you to-day," went on Jack. "And I've rowed three or four miles already."

"Oh, Jack! you are too tired and the sun is too strong," remonstrated Mrs. Ruthven, although inwardly pleased to see the lad stand up for himself.

"I said I never raced with boys," said St. John.

"I would like to see a race," came from Marion. "I dare you to row Jack, St. John."

"Let us make it to the rocks and back," said Jack. "And you can have any of the boats you please. I dare you to do it," and he looked at St. John defiantly.

"St. John may be tired. Perhaps he has been working," suggested Mrs. Ruthven, although she knew better.

"No, he has been walking and resting along shore," said Marion. "We saw him from our boat."

"I'll give you another advantage, besides choice of boats," said Jack, bound that St. John should not back out. "I'll carry Marion as extra weight."

"Oh, that wouldn't be fair!" cried the girl. "Let St. John carry mamma."

"No, I must decline to go," said Mrs. Ruthven.

"I'll take Marion, and St. John need carry only himself," said our hero. "I am certain I can beat him. I dare him to take me up."

There seemed no help for it, so St. John gave in, and soon the three were on the way to Old Ben's boathouse.

CHAPTER XII.

THE BOAT RACE ON THE BAY.

"I think this is a very foolish proceeding," observed St. John as they walked along.

"I think it's going to be lots of fun," replied Marion. "The one who wins shall receive a lovely bunch of roses from me."

"Then I'll win," said the spendthrift, and bestowed a meaning smile upon her, which instantly made her turn her head.

They used a short cut to the beach, consequently they did not meet Old Ben and Dr. Mackey.

When the boathouse was gained they went to inspect the four boats lying there.

St. John knew the boats well, for he was by no means an unskilled rower.

He picked out the lightest of the craft, one which was long and narrow, and also took the best pair of oars.

Marion was going to remonstrate, but Jack silenced her.

"But, Jack, if you have a poor boat, and carry me, too—" she began, in a whisper.

"I'll beat him, anyway," replied our hero. "I know I can do it."

Soon they had the boats out.

Marion half expected St. John to invite her to enter his craft, but in this she was mistaken. The spendthrift was afraid that the extra weight would prove fatal to his success. Yet it angered him to have his cousin go off with Jack.

"Marion, you ought to remain on shore," he said. "The race ought to be rowed with both boats empty."

"Well, if you think best—" she began.

"No, Marion, you are to go with me," put in Jack hastily. "I said I would row with you in my boat, and I will."

"But I am quite a weight—"

"Never mind; jump in."

As there seemed no help for it, Marion entered Jack's boat and our hero pulled a rod away from the shore.

"Now where is the race to be?" asked St. John, as he followed Jack's example and pulled off his coat.

"Let Marion decide that," said the youth promptly.

"Then make it to the Sister Rocks," said Marion. "Each boat must go directly around the rocks."

"That suits me," said Jack.

"It's a good mile and a half," grumbled St. John. He had no desire to exert himself in that warm sun.

"It's no farther for you than for Jack," answered the girl. "Come, are you ready?"

There was a pause, and then St. John said that he was.

"And you, Jack?"

"All ready, Marion."

"Then go!" cried the girl.

The four oars dropped into the water and off went the two boats, side by side.

St. John, eager to win for the sake of finding favor in Marion's eyes, exerted himself to the utmost, and soon forged ahead.

"Oh, Jack! he is going to beat," cried the girl, in disappointment. "I am too much of a load for you."

"The race has but started," he replied. "Wait until we turn the rocks and then see who is ahead."

On and on went the two boats, St. John pulling strongly, but somewhat wildly—a pace he could not keep up. Jack rowed strongly, too, but kept himself somewhat in reserve.

When half the distance to the Sister Rocks was covered St. John was four boat-lengths ahead.

"Ha! what did I tell you!" he cried. "I will beat you, and beat you badly, too!"

"'He laughs best who laughs last,'" quoted Jack. "Marion, sit a little more to the left, please. There, that's it—now we'll go along straighter."

"I wish I could help row," she said. "But that wouldn't be fair. But, oh, Jack! you must beat him!"

Slowly, but surely, they approached the Sister Rocks. Being ahead, St. John turned in, to take the shortest cut around the turning-stake, if such the rocks may be called.

"Too bad, Jack, you will have to go outside," cried Marion.

"Never mind, I'll beat him, anyway," answered our hero, and now let himself out.

The added strength to his stroke soon told, and before long he began to crawl close to St. John's craft. Then he overlapped his opponent and forged ahead.

"Hurrah! you are ahead!" cried Marion excitedly, but in a voice her cousin might not hear. "Keep up, Jack; you are doing wonderfully well."

Our hero did keep up, and when he reached the first of the Sister Rocks he was more than two boat-lengths ahead.

He knew the rocks well, and glided around them skillfully,

with just enough water between the rocks and the boat to make the turning a safe one.

"Now for the home stretch!" he murmured, and began to pull as never before. He felt certain he could defeat St. John, but he wished to make the defeat as large as possible. "He'll find even a nobody can row," he told himself, with grim satisfaction.

To have Jack go ahead of him drove St. John frantic, and as he drew closer to the rocks he became wildly excited.

"He must not win this race—he a mere nobody," he muttered. "What will Marion think if he wins?"

The thought was maddening, and he pulled desperately, first on one oar and then on the other. Around the rocks the waters ran swiftly, and before he knew it there came a crash and his craft was stove in and upset. He clutched at the gunwale of the boat, but missed it, and plunged headlong into the bay.

When the mishap occurred Jack was paying sole attention to the work cut out for him, consequently he did not notice what was taking place. Nor did Marion see the disaster until several seconds later.

"St. John will—" began the girl, and then turned deadly pale. "Oh, Jack!" she screamed.

"What's the matter?" he cried, and stopped rowing instantly.

"Look! look! St. John's boat has gone on the rocks and he is overboard!" she gasped.

"How foolish for him to row so close," was Jack's comment. And then he added, in something like disgust, "I reckon the race is off now."

"We must go back for him," went on Marion. "See, he has disappeared."

The girl was right, the weight of St. John's clothing had carried him beneath the surface. The swiftly running water had likewise caught him, and when he came up it was at a point fifty feet away from the nearest rock.

"He will be drowned, Jack!"

"Help! help!" came in a faint cry from the spendthrift. "Help me, Jack! Don't leave me to perish!"

"Keep up, I'm coming!" answered Jack readily, and as quickly as he could he turned his boat and pulled in the direction where St. John had again sunk from sight.

The spendthrift was but an indifferent swimmer, and the weight of his clothing was much against him. Moreover, he was scared to death, and threw his arms around wildly instead of doing his best to save himself.

He had gone down once, and now, as Jack's boat came closer, he went down a second time.

"Oh, Jack! he will surely be drowned!" gasped Marion, and she placed her hands over her eyes to keep out the awful sight.

"Look to the boat, I am going after him!" cried our hero suddenly, and leaping to the bow, he dove into the bay after the sinking young man.

LEAPING TO THE BOW, HE DOVE INTO THE BAY AFTER THE SINKING YOUNG MAN.—*Page 92.*

He had been afraid of bringing the craft closer and hitting St. John. Now he struck out boldly, and then made a second dive, coming up close to the spendthrift's side.

St. John wished to cry out, but the words would not come. Espying Jack, he grabbed for the lad and clutched him around the throat.

"Don't hold on so tight!" cried Jack in alarm. "I will save you. Take hold of my shoulder."

But St. John was too excited to be reasoned with, and instead of letting up, he clung closer than ever, so that soon both were in peril of going down.

"Let up, I say!" repeated Jack, and then, drawing up one knee, he literally forced the young man from him. Then, as St. John turned partly around, he caught him under the arms and began to tread water.

By this time Marion was at the oars, her temporary fear vanishing with the thought that not only St. John, but also Jack, was in peril. With caution she brought the rowboat closer.

"Catch hold there," said Jack, and seeing the boat, St. John made a wild clutch for the gunwale, nearly upsetting the craft.

"Don't—you'll have me in the water next!" screamed Marion. Then Jack steadied the boat, and St. John scrambled in over the stern, to fall on the bottom all but exhausted, and so frightened that he could not utter a word. Jack followed on board.

"Oh, St. John, what a narrow escape!" gasped Marion, after Jack was safe. "I thought you would surely be drowned!"

For the moment St. John did not speak. He sat up, panting heavily.

"The race is off," said Jack. "Shall I go after your boat, St. John?"

"I don't care," growled the spendthrift, at last. "Where is she?"

"Caught between the rocks."

"Let Old Ben get the boat," put in Marion. "Both of you had better get home with your wet clothing."

"I'm all right," answered the spendthrift coolly.

"St. John, Jack saved your life."

"Oh, I would have been all right—although, to be sure, my boat was wrecked."

"Why, what would you have done?" asked Marion, in astonishment.

"I would have swam to shore, or else crawled on the rocks and signaled Old Ben to come out after me," answered St. John.

He never thought to thank Jack, and this made Marion very indignant.

"Jack did a great deal for you, St. John," she exclaimed. "And he won the race, too," she added, and would say no more.

Without loss of time Jack rowed the boat back to the landing and St. John leaped out. He wished to assist his cousin, but she gave her hand to Jack. Then the three walked toward the plantation in almost utter silence.

CHAPTER XIII.

DR. MACKEY TELLS HIS STORY.

Left to herself, Mrs. Ruthven grew restless and began to walk around the garden, examining the flower beds and the shrubbery.

She did not like what St. John had had to say concerning Marion. While she did not exactly fear the young man, yet she had heard several reports which were not to his credit.

"They say he gambles on horse races," she thought. "And I have heard that the plantation is heavily mortgaged. Perhaps he wishes to marry Marion only for the money she may bring him. And then it is not right for him to remain around here when other men are at the front, serving their country's flag."

She remained in the garden for some time, and was on the point of moving for the house when she saw Old Ben approaching with Dr. Mackey.

"A stranger—and dressed in the uniform of a Confederate," she said, half aloud. "What can he wish here?"

"Good-afternoon, missus," said Old Ben, removing his hat. "Here am a gen'man as wishes to see yo'," and he bowed low.

"To see me?" said Mrs. Ruthven.

"Yes, madam," replied the doctor. "Permit me to introduce myself. I am Dr. Mackey, a surgeon attached to the Fifth Virginia regiment," and he bowed gravely.

"I am happy to make the acquaintance of an officer in our army, sir," replied Mrs. Ruthven, and held out her hand.

"I understand the late Colonel Ruthven was also of our army, and died at a gallant charge on the field of Gettysburg," continued the doctor, as he shook hands.

"You have been correctly informed, doctor."

"De doctor brings most important information, missus," put in old Ben, who was almost exploding to tell what he knew.

"Is that so?" cried Mrs. Ruthven. "What is it?"

"I came to speak to you about yonder wreck on Hemlock Bluff rocks," said the surgeon. "The sight of that wreck has taken me back to the affairs of about eleven years ago."

"So you were—you knew of it at that time, sir?"

"Yes, I was one of the passengers on the ship, madam."

"A passenger! I thought all of the passengers were drowned,—I mean all but those who came ashore here."

"I was not drowned. I was swept overboard before our ship

came into the bay, and clung to a spar for hours, until the storm abated. Then a ship bound for Cuba came along and took me on board and carried me to Havana. The shock and the exposure were too much for me, and when I recovered physically the authorities at the hospital adjudged me insane, and I was placed in an asylum for years. Slowly my reason returned to me, and at last I left the island of Cuba and came to the Southern States. This was shortly after the war had broken out, and, knowing nothing else to do, I offered my services to General Lee, and was accepted and placed in the hospital corps."

"But why did you not come here before?"

"I could not tell exactly where the ship had stranded, and did not hear of the wreck on Hemlock Bluff rocks until about three weeks ago. Then I determined to make an investigation. I have now visited the wreck and have learned positively that it is that of the ship upon which myself, my wife, and our little son took passage."

"Yourself, your wife, and your little son," repeated Mrs. Ruthven, and then of a sudden her breast began to heave. "Your wife and son were with you?"

"Yes, madam."

"Wha—what was your little son's name?" she faltered, hardly able to go on.

"Jack."

"By golly, he must be our Jack's fadder!" burst out Old Ben. "Now don't dat beat de nation!"

"Jack! No! no! You—you cannot be our Jack's father!" cried Mrs. Ruthven.

"I understand you are very much attached to the boy," went on Dr. Mackey smoothly. "It is a pity. Yes, he is truly my son."

The tears came into Mrs. Ruthven's eyes, but she hastily brushed them away. "Jack does not look much like you," she declared.

"That is true, but he bears a strong resemblance to my dead brother Walter, and that is what made me certain he is my son. I saw him in town a day or two ago, although he did not see me."

"This is very strange." The lady hardly knew how to go on. The thought that she might have to give up Jack was a bitter one. "Have you spoken to Jack yet?"

"No. Isn't he here?"

"No, he went for a boat race, against his cousin, St. John Ruthven—I mean my nephew," she stammered.

"Do you expect him back soon?"

"I do not believe he will be gone more than an hour or so."

"Then I will wait."

"Of course, Dr. Mackey. Will you come into the house?"

The surgeon was willing, and the lady led the way. But presently she turned back to beckon to Old Ben.

"Go after Jack at once," she said. "Tell him it is important, but do not say anything more to anybody." Ben nodded, and without further delay strode off.

"I have heard something of how the wreck struck here and how my poor wife was cast ashore with Jack in her arms," said the doctor, as he threw himself into an easy-chair. "I should be very much gratified to receive the particulars from your lips. Did my wife have anything to say?"

"Nothing much, sir. She was delirious up to the moment of her death."

"Poor, dear Julia!" murmured the surgeon, and bringing out his handkerchief, he wiped his eyes with much affectation.

"Was her name Julia?" asked Mrs. Ruthven curiously.

"Yes, madam." The doctor looked up suddenly. "What makes you ask?"

"It ran in my mind that before your wife died she murmured something about her name being Laura."

"Poor dear! she was truly out of her mind," replied the surgeon. "But it is not to be wondered at—considering what happened to me." And he proceeded to make use of his handkerchief again.

Mrs. Ruthven sank into a chair and gave herself up to bitter reflection. What if this man should take Jack from her? The plantation would seem very lonely without him.

Voices were now heard in the garden, and looking out of the window the lady of the house saw Jack approaching, accompanied by Marion and Old Ben. St. John had taken himself off, in order to get home and exchange his wet clothing for dry garments.

"Oh, Jack! what does this mean?" cried Mrs. Ruthven when she saw that our hero was dripping wet.

"He saved St. John's life, mamma," exclaimed Marion.

"Saved St. John's life?"

"Yes. St. John's boat struck on the rocks, and he went overboard. The current was strong, and he would have been swept away only Jack leaped overboard and went to his assistance."

"You noble boy!" murmured Mrs. Ruthven, and as he came in, by way of one of the long veranda windows, she caught him by both hands.

"Old Ben said you wished to see me," replied Jack, and then he caught sight of Dr. Mackey and his face fell. "The man I had the row with," he thought.

"Jack, this is Dr. Mackey," said Mrs. Ruthven, in strained tones. "He—he came here to see you." She could get no further.

"To see me? What for?"

"My boy, I am pleased to meet you," said the doctor, rising and extending his hand. And he then added in a lower voice, "How like Walter! How very like Walter!"

"I—I don't understand you," stammered Jack. "What do you want of me?"

"My boy, you are thinking of that encounter we had on the bridge. Let us both forget it. I came here on a most important mission. Jack, I am your father!"

"My father?" And our hero leaped back in astonishment.

"Yes, my son, I am your father." Dr. Mackey caught our hero by the hand. "No doubt the news seems strange to you. Nevertheless, it is true."

Jack hardly heard the latter words, for his head was in a swim. This crafty-looking, overbearing individual his parent? The shock was an awful one. He turned to his foster mother.

"Mother, is this true—is this man my real father?" he cried beseechingly.

"So he claims," returned Mrs. Ruthven.

"My dear, dear son, I trust you do not disbelieve me," said the doctor, in an apparently hurt tone of voice.

"I—I don't know what to say," faltered Jack. "This is so strange—so unexpected. Why didn't you come here before?"

"I have just been telling Mrs. Ruthven my story," and the surgeon repeated what he had said, with several added details. As the man went on our hero's face grew very pale, and he moved slowly towards Mrs. Ruthven and clutched her by the shoulder.

"Mother, I don't want to leave you!" he whispered hoarsely. "I don't like this man, even if he is my father!"

"I do not want you to leave me, Jack," she answered, embracing him in spite of the fact that he was dripping wet. "But if this man is really your father—"

"Make him prove it!"

"You will not take his word?"

"No! no! I do not like his looks. He is the man who met me on the bridge and treated me like a slave."

Marion had listened to the conversation with a look of horror slowly rising on her face. Now she rushed toward Jack.

"Jack, can this be true, and must I give you up?" she sobbed.

"No, I'm not going to give you up, Marion. We have always been brother and sister, and so we shall remain—if you are willing."

"Yes, dear Jack; stay by all means."

By this time Dr. Mackey had arisen to his feet, and now he came up to Jack with a darkening face.

"Did I understand you to say that you wished me to prove I was your father?" he demanded harshly.

"Yes, I do wish you to prove it," answered Jack, with a boldness born of desperation. "And until you prove it I shall remain here—if Mrs. Ruthven will let me."

"By golly, dat's de talk!" came from Old Ben, who was hanging around on the veranda.

"Shut up, you worthless nigger!" cried the doctor, at which Ben disappeared like magic.

"This is a very—ahem—a very strange way to treat a newly found father, Jack."

"I don't acknowledge you as my father."

"Ha! you won't believe me?"

"I will not, sir, and until you prove your claim in court I shall remain with the lady who has been a real mother to me," answered our hero pointedly and firmly.

CHAPTER XIV.

JACK SPEAKS HIS MIND.

A dead silence followed our hero's declaration to remain with Mrs. Ruthven until Dr. Mackey had proved his claim to Jack in a court of law.

"This is a fine way to talk!" ejaculated the surgeon at last. "A fine way, truly!"

"I mean what I say!" declared Jack. "Mother, am I right or wrong?" And he turned pleadingly to Mrs. Ruthven.

"Dr. Mackey will certainly have to establish his claim to you before I give you up, Jack," replied the lady of the plantation quickly. "You see, I have adopted him legally, and he has been as dear to me as though he were my own flesh and blood."

"Well—er—of course, in one way, your decision does you credit, madam," answered the surgeon lamely. "You have done a great deal for the lad, and for that I must be as thankful as he is. When I have proved my claim I will pay you back all the money you have spent upon him."

"I shall not wish a cent, sir."

"Yet I shall insist, madam."

"Are you wealthy?" asked Marion curiously.

"Yes, Miss Ruthven—or I will be as soon as I have proven my identity. As yet I have been able to do but little. Let me add, Mackey is not my real name."

"What is your real name?" questioned Mrs. Ruthven.

"I will reveal that later, when I have taken the proper steps in law to obtain the vast property which is rightfully coming to me. You see, when I disappeared, so to speak, nearly eleven years ago, my property went into the hands of distant relatives, and they hate to give it up, and are just as anxious to prove me an impostor as you seem to be."

"I am not anxious to prove you an impostor, Dr. Mackey; my heart is wrapped up in Jack, that is all. If he is your son, I will rejoice that he will be well off."

"I don't want to be rich; I would rather stay with you," put in our hero quickly, and he meant what he said.

"Your affection for your foster mother does you credit, Jack," said the doctor smoothly.

"She has been the best of mothers to me; so why shouldn't I love her?"

"True, my son, true. But it is strange that you have no warm feeling for me—such as I have for you."

"You are a stranger to me."

"I trust your feeling towards me changes, for I want my only son to love me."

At this Jack was silent, and instead of looking at the man he looked at Mrs. Ruthven and at Marion. Then, unable to control his feelings, he rushed from the room, mounted the stairs, and burst into his own apartment, where he threw himself on the bed, wet as he was, to give himself up to his misery.

"I don't want that man for a father!" he cried, over and over again, half tearfully and with set teeth. "I don't want him! He isn't a bit like anybody I could love! Oh, how I wish I had never set eyes on him!"

"It is a great shock to Jack, and to all of us," was Mrs. Ruthven's comment, after the lad was gone.

"My reception here has been a great shock to me," said the doctor bluntly. "My own son runs away from me."

"He had some trouble with you a couple of weeks ago."

"Pooh, that was nothing! I had almost forgotten it."

"Jack does not forget such things easily. Moreover, he is slow to make friends with anybody."

"He doesn't know the chances he is throwing away. Were it not that he is my son, and my heart goes out toward him, I would never bother him."

"What chances has he?" asked Marion.

"I shall be very rich; and, not only that, our family has a famous name in England, with a title attached. Jack may some day be a nobleman."

"I reckon he'd rather be an American," answered Marion.

"Well, there is no accounting for tastes," said the surgeon dryly. "And you evidently have him well drilled in."

"What actual proofs have you that Jack is your son?" asked Mrs. Ruthven, after a painful pause.

"I have a number of private papers; also the marriage certificate which proves that I married Jack's mother. More than that, I expect soon to meet an old college chum who knows much of the past, and who can testify in my behalf."

"Well, on my own account and on Jack's, I feel that I must make you prove your claim, Dr. Mackey. It will be hard enough to give up the boy when I am assured that he is really your own."

"I will not discuss the situation further," cried the doctor, moving stiffly toward the door. "But unless you wish me to take immediate steps to take Jack from you, you must make me one promise."

"And what is that, sir?"

"That you will not spirit the boy away from this plantation, so that he cannot be brought into court when wanted."

"I will promise that. I do not wish to do anything contrary to law."

"Then that is all for the present, Mrs. Ruthven, and I will bid you good-day."

"When do you expect to come back again?"

"As soon as my duties will permit. The Yankees are pressing us hard, and I cannot neglect my duties as a surgeon in our army."

In a moment more the doctor was gone. Mrs. Ruthven watched him out of sight, then sank in a chair, all but overcome. Old Ben saw her and came up, hat in hand, his honest face full of genuine grief.

"Missus, dis am de worst wot I eber did heah," he said. "De idea, dat dat man wants to take our Jack away! It am dreadful!"

"Yes, Ben; I do not know how I can endure it."

"He don't look like Jack one bit; not one bit, missus!"

"I know it, Ben. He says Jack resembles his brother Walter."

"Maybe he dun nebber had a brudder Walter."

"Evidently you do not believe him?"

"No, I don't."

"Where did you meet him?"

"He cum to de boathouse, and got me to row him ober to de wrack."

"You took him there. What did he want at the wreck?"

"I dunno dat, missus. He tole me to go away fer an hour or so. He went below in de wrack, out ob sight."

"Perhaps he was after something belonging to the past. Did he bring anything away with him?"

"I aint suah about dat, missus. When I rowed him ashore he had a tin box hidden away under his coat, but he might have had dat when I took him ober."

"How large a box?"

"About dis size," and Ben held out his hands.

"He wouldn't be likely to take such a box to the wreck with him. He must have found it on the ship," went on Mrs. Ruthven, with interest.

"Where could he find it, missus? De folks around yeah has tuk everyt'ing off dat wrack long ago."

"Perhaps not. To tell the truth, Ben, I do not like that man's manner at all."

"No more do I, missus. He's got a bad eye, he has," responded the colored man warmly.

"If you see him again, Ben, I wish you would watch him closely."

"I will do it, missus. Yo' can trust Ole Ben."

"You may be able to learn something important."

"If I do, I'll bring de news to yo' directly, missus."

"Perhaps you had better follow him now," went on Mrs. Ruthven suddenly. "If he goes to the battlefield, you can come back."

"I will, missus," and in a moment more Ben was off.

Meanwhile Marion had gone up to Jack's room and knocked on the door. At first there was no answer, and the girl knocked again.

"Who is it?" came in a half-choked voice.

"It is I, Marion. Can't I come in?"

"Yes," answered Jack, and Marion entered the room and sat down beside our hero on the bed.

"Oh, Jack, I'm so sorry for you!" was all she could say.

"Marion, do you honestly think that man is my father?" he questioned anxiously.

"I don't know what to say, Jack. It's all so strange."

"If he was my father it seems to me I ought to feel differently toward him."

"Perhaps it's the shock, Jack."

"No, it isn't. I could never love that man as a son ought to love his father," went on our hero impetuously.

"Hush! you mustn't talk so!"

"I can't help it. I hated that man when we met on the bridge—and—and I hate him still!"

"Oh, Jack!"

"It's true, Marion. I don't see why he wanted to come here. I was happy enough, with you and mother."

"He hasn't taken you away yet, Jack. Mother will make him prove his claim first, never fear. She feels as badly almost as do you."

"To me the whole story sounds unreasonable, Marion. If there is a big fortune in the background, that man may only be scheming to get it."

"But, if that is true, why doesn't he ignore you and keep the money for himself?"

"I don't know—excepting it may be that he wants me in order

to make his claim stronger, or something like that. I don't know much about law."

"Neither do I. But if it comes to the worst, mother will get a lawyer and make that man prove everything he says."

The two talked the matter over for a while, and gradually Jack grew calmer. But look at it from every possible light, he could not make himself believe that Dr. Mackey was his father.

Presently Mrs. Ruthven entered the chamber and also sat down to comfort our hero.

"He is certainly a strange man," said she, referring to the surgeon. "He went to the wreck and was aboard alone for some time, so Old Ben tells me."

"What did he do?"

"Ben doesn't know."

"I shall visit the wreck again before long and make a search," said Jack.

The three talked the matter over for several hours, but reached no further conclusions. Jack expected the doctor back the next day, but he did not appear, nor did he show himself for some time to come. In the meantime things of great importance happened.

CHAPTER XV.

CAPTAIN JACK AT THE FRONT.

Two days after the conversation recorded in the last chapter the folks living at the Ruthven plantation were disturbed at daybreak by the distant firing of cannon, which continued for over two hours, gradually drawing closer and closer.

"What can this mean?" asked Mrs. Ruthven, in alarm, as she moved to the window. "Can the Yankees be pressing our army back again?"

"I will take the spyglass and go to the roof," said Jack. "Perhaps I'll be able to see something."

Armed with the glass he made his way to the garret of the plantation home, and then up a ladder leading to a scuttle of the roof. Marion, as anxious as anybody, came after him.

Standing on the roof, Jack adjusted the spyglass and gave a long look in the direction from whence the sounds were proceeding.

"What do you see, Jack?"

"I can see nothing but smoke," he answered. "Some is over at Bannock's woods and the other near Townley church."

"Don't you see any of our soldiers?"

"No. The trees are in the way, and all I can see is a stretch of the bay road. Hark! the cannon are at it again!"

"But the sounds are closer," persisted Marion.

"That is true. They must be—hullo! there come our men, along the bottom of the woods—they are retreating!"

"Do you mean to say they are coming this way, Jack?"

"Yes, Marion. See for yourself!" And he handed the girl the spyglass.

Marion took a long look, and gave a sigh. "You are right, our brave soldiers are suffering another defeat. Perhaps they will come to our plantation!"

"If they do, we ought to do all we can for the wounded," answered Jack quickly.

"To be sure. Oh, see! they are running this way as fast as they can—fully two regiments of them!"

Again Jack took the glass. "Yes, and now I can see the Yankees. My, what a lot of them! At least twice as many men as there are on our side. I really believe they are going to push on to here, Marion!"

At this the girl turned pale. "And if they do?"

"We must defend ourselves as best we can," answered Jack. "Do you know what I am going to do? Call out the Home Guard!"

"But, Jack, you may be shot down?"

"If I am, it will be only at my post of duty, Marion."

So speaking, Jack leaped down the ladder into the garret and ran downstairs. He met Old Ben just coming into the house, accompanied by Darcy Gilbert.

"Darcy! just the fellow I want to see! And Old Ben, too!"

"The Yankees are coming!" answered Darcy.

"I know it, Darcy. I was going to call out the Home Guard."

"Exactly my idea."

"Old Ben can help you get the boys together."

"'Deed I will, Massah Jack, if yo' wants me to," responded the colored man.

Darcy and Ben were soon off and Jack re-entered the house, to be confronted by Mrs. Ruthven.

"What are you up to, Jack?"

"I have called out our Home Guard, mother. The Yankees shall not destroy this plantation or molest you and Marion."

"You must do nothing rash, Jack."

"I will be careful. But this is private property, and you and Marion are ladies, and our enemy must remember this," responded Jack, and ran off to don his uniform and his sword.

Inside of half an hour the members of Jack's company began to appear, until there were nineteen boys assembled. Each had his gun or his pistol fully loaded, and the appearance made by the lads, when drawn up in a line, was quite an imposing one.

"Ise got a pistol," said Old Ben, showing a long, old-fashioned "hoss" pistol on the sly. "If anybody tries to shoot Massah Jack, he will heah from dis darky, suah."

"Thank you, Ben," answered our hero. "You always were true to me. If ever I grow up to be a man and get rich, I shan't forget you," and this made Old Ben grin from ear to ear.

Presently there was a clatter on the road beyond the plantation, and a Confederate battery, drawn by horses covered with foam, swept past.

"The Yanks are coming!" was the cry. "Get indoors and hide your jewelry and silverware!"

"They are coming!" muttered our hero. He called the boys together. "Home Guard, attention!" he cried out. "Line up here. Carry arms! Boys, are you willing to stand by me and help me to keep my mother's house from being ransacked?"

"Yes! yes!" was the ready reply.

"Hurrah for Captain Jack!" put in several of the more enthusiastic ones.

"Thank you, boys. We won't fight unless we have to. But if it comes to that, let everybody give a good account of himself."

"We will! We will!"

Soon another battery swept by the house, the horses almost ready to drop from exhaustion. Marion saw this and whispered to her mother.

"Let me do it, mother," she pleaded.

"If you so much wish it," answered Mrs. Ruthven.

With all speed the girl ran to the barn and brought out her own horse, a beautiful black, and ran him to the road.

"Take my horse and hitch him to yonder cannon!" she cried. "He is fresh—he will help you save the piece!"

"Good fer you, young lady!" shouted one of the cannoneers. "We've got friends yet, it seems!" The horse was taken, and the cannon moved on at a swifter pace than ever.

"That was grand of you, Marion!" cried Jack. He knew just how much she thought of the steed she had sacrificed, her pet saddle horse.

And now came several of the hospital corps, carrying the wounded on stretchers, and also several ambulances. In the meantime the shooting came closer and closer, and several shells sped over the plantation, to burst with a crash in the woods beyond.

"The battle is at hand! God defend us!" murmured Mrs. Ruthven.

Several Confederates with stretchers were crossing the lawn. On the stretchers lay three soldiers, all badly wounded.

"We can't carry them any further, madam," said one of the party. "Will you be kind enough to take them in?"

"Yes, yes!" cried Mrs. Ruthven. "Bring them in at once. We will do our best for them!" And she summoned the servants to prepare cots on the lower floor, since it would have been awkward to take the wounded upstairs.

The stretcher-carriers were followed by others, until six wounded Confederates lay on cots in the sitting room. A young surgeon was at hand, and he went to work without delay, and Mrs. Ruthven and Marion assisted.

And now the army was passing by the plantation, some on foot, some on horseback, and all exhausted, ragged, covered with dust and dirt, and many badly wounded. The shooting of small-arms had ceased, but the distant cannon still kept booming, and occasionally a shell burst in the vicinity. As the last of the Confederates swept by Jack ran down to the roadway.

"The enemy are coming!" he said, after a long look ahead. "They will be here in less than ten minutes."

Soon the trampling of horses' hoofs was heard, and then came the occasional blast of a trumpet. At last a troop of cavalry swept by, paying no attention to the Ruthven homestead.

The cavalry was followed at a distance by a company of rascally looking guerrillas—followers of every army—who fight simply for the sake of looting afterward.

"To the house!" cried the captain of the guerrillas, a man named Sandy Barnes.

"Company, attention!" cried out Jack, and drew up his command across the lawn in front of the homestead.

"Halt!" shouted Captain Barnes. And then he added; "What are you boys doing here?"

"We are the guard of this house," answered Jack, quietly but firmly.

"Guard nothin'! Out of our way!" growled the guerrilla.

"We will not get out of your way, and you will advance at your peril."

"What, will you boys show fight?" queried the guerrilla curiously.

"We will!" came from the boys. "Keep back!"

"This is private property and must be respected," went on Jack. "Besides, the house is now a hospital, for there are six wounded Confederates inside, in charge of a surgeon."

The guerrilla muttered something under his breath.

"Come on, anyhow!" shouted somebody in a rear rank. "It looks like a house worth visitin'!"

"Try to enter the house and we will shoot!" went on Jack, his face growing white.

"Why, youngster, you don't know who you are talking to," growled Barnes.

He stepped forward as if to enter the house by a side door, when Jack ran in front of him and raised his sword.

"Not another step, if you value your life!"

"Out of my way, boy!" And now the guerrilla raised his own sword, while some of his men raised their guns.

It was truly a trying moment, and Marion, at the window, looked on with bated breath. "Oh, if Jack should be killed!" she thought.

But now there came a shout from the road, and there appeared a regiment of regular Federal troops. The guerrillas saw them coming, and gazed anxiously at their leader.

"It's Colonel Stanton's regiment!" muttered a guerrilla lieutenant. "He won't stand no nonsense, cap."

"I know it," growled Barnes. "Right face, forward march!" he shouted, and, as quickly as they had come, the guerrillas left the plantation and took to a side road leading to the distant hills.

But the Federal regiment had seen them, and as the guerrillas ran they received a volley which lay several of them low. They were virtually outlaws, and knew it, and lost no time in getting out of sight.

"Halt!" shouted the Federal colonel as he rode up across the lawn, and one after another the companies behind him stopped in their march. Then the Northerner came closer to Jack and the others of the Home Guard.

"What's the matter here? What does this mean?"

Jack gazed up into the face of the Federal colonel and saw that it was an unusually kindly one. "We are defending this home, sir; that's all. I reckon those fellows who just ran off wanted to ransack it."

"The scoundrels! I've been after them twice before. Was anybody hurt?"

"No, sir."

"You are a young Confederate, I presume?"

"I am the captain of these boys. We call ourselves the Home Guard. We wish to protect our homes, that's all."

At this the face of the colonel broke out into a warm smile.

"You do yourself credit, my lad. You could not do better than protect your homes and your mothers and sisters. Whose place is this?"

"Mrs. Alice Ruthven's."

"Did the Confederate battery just retreat past here?"

"I cannot answer that question, sir."

"Well, it doesn't matter much. We have got them on the run, and that was all we wanted for the present."

"I hope you don't intend to do anything to this place," went on Jack anxiously. "It is private property, and, besides, we have six wounded men here, in charge of a surgeon."

"An officer who is a gentleman always respects private property," was the grave answer. "As long as you do nothing treacherous, you have nothing to fear from me or my men." And so speaking, the colonel rode back to the road.

"A fine-looking man, and a gentleman, if ever there was one," thought Jack. "What a difference between him and that fellow who threatened me with his sword!"

"Will they come back, Jack?" asked Mrs. Ruthven, as she came outside.

"I don't know, mother. But the officer said we had nothing to fear."

"He looked like an honest gentleman."

"So I thought. How are those wounded men making out?"

"One is already dead, poor fellow. But the surgeon has hopes of the others."

"Is Marion helping the doctor?"

"Yes. I want her to come away from the awful sights, but she will not. Jack, she is almost as brave as you are!"

"Pooh! I'm not so brave, mother."

"Yes, you are. Why, that rascal was going to run you through with his sword!"

"Dat he was," put in Old Ben. "But let me tell yo' sumt'ing, missus. I had dat feller covered wid dis hoss-pistol ob mine. If he had tried to slew Jack dat would hab been de end of the rascal, suah pop!"

"Good for you, Ben! Continue to look out for Jack, and I will reward you handsomely," concluded Mrs. Ruthven, and returned to the house.

CHAPTER XVI.

COLONEL STANTON'S VISIT.

The Federal regiment went into camp up the road, but a short distance from the Ruthven home. The coming of the soldiers filled the whole neighborhood with alarm, but it was soon evident that Colonel Stanton was a strict disciplinarian and did not countenance any pilfering, and then the inhabitants became more quiet. In the meanwhile the Confederate troops had departed for parts unknown. But another battle was not far off.

Attached to Colonel Stanton's regiment was a young man named Harry Powell, a surgeon, who was a nephew to Mrs. Ruthven, although the two had not seen each other for years. Powell was a fine fellow, and well liked by all who knew him, the single exception to the case being St. John Ruthven, who was too much of a sneak to admire anybody so free-hearted and manly.

Harry Powell had drifted to the North several years before, and established a practice in Philadelphia. He was thoroughly opposed to slavery, and when the war broke out lost no time in joining the Federal troops, much to the horror of his two aunts and his cousin Marion. As for St. John, that spendthrift said it was "just like Harry, who had no head on his shoulders, anyway."

On the day following the arrival of the Federal troops Old Ben was making his way to his cabin for some things, when he ran across Colonel Stanton on his way to the Ruthven mansion. The colonel was accompanied by Harry Powell, but the young surgeon now wore a heavy mustache, and for the moment the old colored man did not recognize him.

"See here, my man. I want to talk to you," began Colonel Stanton, as he held up his hand for Ben to halt.

"Yes, sah," and Old Ben touched his hat respectfully.

"Did I understand that this is the plantation of Mrs. Alice Ruthven?"

"Yes, sah."

"Why, it's Old Ben!" cried Harry Powell, striding forward. "Don't you remember me, you old rascal?" and he slapped the colored man on the back.

Old Ben stared in astonishment for a moment, and then his ebony face broke out into a broad smile.

"Bless my soul, if it aint Massah Harry Powell!"

"Of course it is, Ben."

"Yo' is so changed I didn't know yo', sah."

"I suppose I am changed, Ben. Is my aunt at home?"

"Yes, sah."

"Good. I want very much to see her."

Old Ben shook his head dubiously.

"Massah Harry, yo' aint gwine an' joined de Yanks, hab yo'?" he questioned.

"Yes, Ben; I am fighting for the old flag."

"Yo' aunt an' Miss Marion will be wery sorry to heah dat, sah."

"I presume so. But that cannot be helped. I did as my heart dictated, Ben. I want to see all colored folks free, as you are."

"Dat would be wery nice certainly, sah, but—but—"

"It was too bad we had to fight, you mean." Harry Powell looked up. "Who is that coming?"

"Dat am Massah Jack, sah?"

"Oh! Why, when I was here before he was nothing but a little shaver." The young surgeon raised his voice. "Hullo, Jack! come here."

Wondering who it was who was calling him so familiarly, Jack came forward. He started back upon seeing Harry Powell, and in a Federal uniform.

"You!" he cried.

"Yes, Jack. Come, won't you shake hands with me?" and the young surgeon smiled good-naturedly.

"Well—that is—I don't like to shake hands with a—a Yankee," stammered Jack.

"Oh, so you object to my uniform?"

"I do, Harry. Why did you join the Yankees?"

"Because I thought it best. If you won't shake hands with me as a Yankee, won't you shake hands as a cousin?"

At this our hero's face relaxed, for he had always liked Harry Powell immensely.

"Yes, I'll do that," he said, and they shook hands warmly.

"And how is your mother these days, Jack?"

"Quite well, but a good deal alarmed."

"She need not be alarmed because of us, Jack. Is that not so, Colonel Stanton?"

The colonel bowed. His manner was so pleasant that Jack felt more drawn to him than ever.

"You are kind," he said. "I thought all Yankees were brutes."

"They are far from that, Jack. But I was going to ask, can I see my aunt?"

"I suppose so. But she'll be hurt to see you in that uniform."

"Never mind, I'll risk that," rejoined Harry Powell.

Old Ben continued on his way, and Jack and the others walked toward the Ruthven plantation. Then our hero ran ahead, to tell Mrs. Ruthven of the visitors.

"A fine, manly young fellow, Powell," remarked Colonel Stanton, when he and the young surgeon were left alone.

"Yes, he has turned out a first-rate lad, colonel."

"I presume, were he older, he would be at the head of a regular Confederate command, instead of being at the head of this boyish Home Guard."

"Undoubtedly, sir. But I am glad he is not in the regular ranks."

"Why?"

"I should hate to fight against him, sir."

"I see. Well, this war has brought brother against brother, and worse. To tell the truth, I heartily wish it was over, myself."

In a few minutes more Mrs. Ruthven appeared, her face full of sorrow. As she approached Harry Powell, the tears stood in her eyes.

"My dear aunt, how glad I am to see you, after this long separation!" cried the young man impulsively.

"Oh, Harry! Harry! How can you come here in that uniform?" she returned.

"Let us speak of that later, Aunt Alice. Allow me to introduce you to my superior, Colonel Stanton."

Mrs. Ruthven looked at the colonel steadily, and he bowed gravely. Each saw that the other was of good blood and breeding. The lady of the plantation dropped her eyes.

"Colonel Stanton, courtesy bids me say you are welcome, but—I beg you to consider that I am a Southern woman," she faltered.

"I hope, Mrs. Ruthven, you will not look upon me as an enemy."

"Are you not in arms against my country?"

"Against your section, yes, but not against your country, madam. I fight under the flag which belongs alike to the South and the North."

At this Mrs. Ruthven shook her head sadly.

"I cannot agree with you, sir. But let that drop. May I ask the news? Have our troops been hopelessly defeated?"

"I cannot answer you, Mrs. Ruthven. Our side has won a battle and the Confederate troops have taken to the mountain side. They may engage us again before long."

"Your troops are encamped but a short distance from here, I believe?"

"It is true."

"Are we to consider ourselves as prisoners of war?"

"By no means, Mrs. Ruthven. I am informed that your house is something of a hospital. Let it remain so."

"Thank you."

"You certainly did not expect ill treatment, did you?" went on the colonel curiously.

"You seem to be a gentleman, I must admit, but I have heard such stories of violence and rapine that I have some reasons to be apprehensive."

"The stories are in most cases baseless and without truth. I hope you are not prejudiced enough to think that Federal officers are destitute of honor and humanity. Every true soldier, no matter under what banner he draws his sword, respects a lady, and would be the last to injure or annoy her."

"I can believe that of you, sir, but you are an exception."

"I cannot accept the compliment. I know many of my brother officers, and I am glad to say that what is true of me is true also of them."

"But your President, Mr. Lincoln, I am told is a cruel monster, intent upon the destruction of the South."

"You are sadly misinformed, Mrs. Ruthven. There never beat a warmer, kinder heart than that of Abraham Lincoln, I know, for I have seen him and spoken with him, and I know that no one sorrows more over the stricken homes and bloodshed of this unhappy strife. He is misjudged now, but posterity will do him justice."

"I cannot believe it. If he deplores the evils of war, why does he not end it at once, and order his hordes of Yankee invaders to throw down their arms?"

"Because the life of the nation is at stake. I do not wish to speak severely of your leaders. They are actuated by a mistaken sense of right. Amid the clash of arms, Reason is silent. We are fighting, not against the South, but for its best good."

"You plead well, Colonel Stanton, but I am not convinced," answered the lady of the house.

At that moment Jack came up again, bringing Marion.

"Marion!" cried Harry Powell, and ran up to her.

"Harry!" she returned, and put out her hand to him.

"Will you shake hands with a Yankee?" he asked. "Jack was

rather backward about doing it."

"I am always ready to shake hands with my cousin," she returned, and blushed.

Colonel Stanton was then introduced, and a minute later Harry Powell asked about St. John Ruthven.

"Is he in the ranks, aunt?" he questioned.

"He is not," answered Mrs. Ruthven, and drew down her mouth.

"He cannot leave his mother," put in Marion contemptuously.

"Evidently you think he ought to go?"

"He is a strong, able-bodied man. I would go, were I in his place."

"So would I," put in Jack.

"Then he isn't very patriotic."

"Oh, yes he is—in words," returned Marion. "But in deeds—" She shrugged her pretty shoulders, and that meant a good deal.

Colonel Stanton and Mrs. Ruthven entered the house, followed by Jack, and presently Marion and the young surgeon found themselves alone in the garden.

CHAPTER XVII.

A SCENE IN THE SUMMERHOUSE.

In years gone by Marion and Harry Powell, as little girl and boy, had thought a good deal of each other.

Now, as the pair faced once more, much of the old feelings came back, and pretty Marion found herself blushing deeply, she could not tell exactly why.

She despised Harry's uniform, yet she felt that he looked remarkably handsome in it, and not such an awful bear of a Yankee, after all. The manliness of the young surgeon's superior had likewise made a deep impression upon her.

Before going into the house Mrs. Ruthven had invited the young man to remain to dinner, and he had readily accepted the invitation. But he was by no means anxious to go into the house with the others.

"It is so nice and cool in the garden, Marion," he said. "Let us remain out here for a while, if you have no objections."

"As you will, Harry. But we need not stand. Let us go down to the old summerhouse. Of course you remember that place."

"To be sure, Marion—I remember it only too well. How you used to bring in the flowers and make bouquets and wreaths, and open a flower store and bid me buy—"

"And you wouldn't buy, more than half the time," she laughed. "You always were somewhat contrary, Harry. Is that what made you turn Yankee?"

"I hardly think so. I want to see all the slaves set free."

"Is that all?"

"Isn't that enough?"

"Most Yankees want to see the South broken up and ruined."

"No! no! That is a mistake."

The summerhouse was soon gained, and she sat down, and without ceremony he took a seat on the bench at her side.

"This takes me back ten or fifteen years," he declared, as he looked around at the familiar surroundings. "There are the same old magnolias, with the swing, and the same old rose bush, or new ones just like the old. Marion, you ought to be happy here."

"I was—until the war broke out, and poor papa was killed."

"Yes, that was a shock, and I felt it too, when the news reached me. He was a noble man, Marion."

"So they all say, Harry, but that does not give him back to us.

And now another danger threatens us."

"Another danger? You mean the presence of our troops here? Marion, no harm shall come to you, if I can prevent it."

"But I do not mean that. It is concerning Jack."

"What of your brother?"

"Oh, Harry, he is just like a brother to me, and mamma thinks of him as her son! Now a stranger has appeared on the scene, and he wants to take Jack away from us."

"A stranger. Who?"

"A Confederate surgeon named Dr. Mackey. He claims that he is Jack's father."

"But is he?"

"We do not believe that he is. But he says he can prove it."

"This is news certainly, Marion. Will you give me the particulars?"

"I will," and she did so, to which Harry Powell listened with keen interest.

"Humph! And Jack does not like the man?"

"No, he despises him."

"That will make it awkward, if this doctor's story is true."

"He will have to bring strong proofs to make me believe the story, I can tell you that."

"I do not blame you, Marion." The young surgeon mused for a moment. "It runs in my mind that I have heard of this Dr. Mackey before."

"Where?"

"I cannot remember now. But I believe it was while I was practicing in Philadelphia."

"Was he a doctor there?"

"It runs in my mind that he was connected with some bogus medical institute which defrauded people through the mails. But I am not certain."

"If there is truth in this, I wish you would look the matter up, Harry. Mamma will want to know all she can of Dr. Mackey before she gives up Jack to him."

"I will do my best for you, Marion. I love Jack, too—although he was very young when I went away, if you will remember."

"You have been away a long time, Harry," she replied, and drew a long breath.

"That is true, and I realize it now, although I did not before." He gazed steadily into her face and suddenly caught her hand. "Dear cousin, cannot you forgive me for going over to the enemy?" he pleaded.

She flushed up. "I ought not to, Harry, but—but—"

"You will, nevertheless?"

"I—I will think of it," she faltered.

"We were very intimate when I went away. I would not wish that intimacy broken off."

"Were we intimate?" she murmured shyly.

"Yes, indeed. Don't you remember it? You used to sit in my lap."

"How shocking!" she cried. "Are you sure?"

"As if I could forget it."

"You seem to have an awfully good memory for some things," she said slowly.

"I remember something more, Marion. We were like brother and sister in those days, and you used to put your arms around my neck and kiss me."

"I don't believe I ever did anything so dreadful, Harry!"

"I remember it perfectly well."

"Don't you think we had better go into the house now?"

"Don't get angry, Marion. But—but—I always did think a lot of you, and always shall—even if I have turned Yankee."

"Yankee or not, Harry, you will always be very dear to me as my cousin," she returned hastily.

"Speaking of cousins, does St. John come here often?"

"Yes, quite often."

"I suppose he comes to see you?"

"He comes to see mamma and me. He and Jack are not very good friends."

"What, doesn't Jack like him?"

"He considers St. John overbearing, and St. John thinks Jack an intruder, and possibly of low parentage."

"Is St. John married yet?"

"No."

"And he comes here quite often, you say?"

"Yes."

"Perhaps he is going—that is, he would like to marry you, Marion," blurted out Harry Powell.

At this the girl flushed crimson.

"Well—he has spoken something of it," she replied, in a low voice.

"The dickens he has!"

"Cousin Harry!"

"I beg your pardon, Marion, but—but—this is not pleasant news."

"You mustn't get rough, Harry. St. John says there are no true gentlemen among the Yankees. But I think differently—now I have met Colonel Stanton."

"Oh, confound St. John! There are truer gentlemen among my fellow officers than he will ever be." Harry Powell took a turn around the summerhouse. "But I forgot. I ought not to have spoken so of your future husband."

"Who said he was my intended husband?"

"Why, you intimated as much."

"I am sure I did not."

"It is the same thing. You said he had spoken of marriage to you."

"That is a very different matter."

Harry Powell took another turn around the summerhouse. "I suppose you love him, though I don't understand how any girl could love such an insufferable bore."

"Harry, aren't you prejudiced against St. John?"

"Perhaps I am. But seriously, Marion, what can you find to admire in St. John?"

"He is a Ruthven."

"That is true."

"If I married him I would still remain a Ruthven."

"Then why not remain an old maid and likewise a Ruthven? It would be far better, take my word on it."

"Then you don't advise me to marry?"

"I don't advise you to marry St. John."

"Oh!"

"Are you engaged to him?" he asked, coming closer.

"I am not."

"I am glad to hear it."

"Are you married, Cousin Harry?" she asked suddenly.

"Me? No, Marion—not yet."

"I suppose you'll marry some Yankee girl one of these days."

"I don't think so, unless—"

"Unless what?"

"Unless the girl I always did love goes back on me, Marion. Do you think she will go back on me?" and he caught both of her hands in his own.

"Harry, you are a—a—Yankee."

"But that doesn't affect my feelings for you."

"A true Yankee ought not to care for a Southern girl."

"And why not?"

"Well, I don't know exactly. But it doesn't seem right."

"Do you mean to say that a Southern girl ought not to care for the man who is fighting as his conscience dictates?" he demanded, turning a trifle pale.

"No, no, Harry! I honor you for sticking to your principles. But we had better say no more at present on this subject." She glanced down the garden path. "See, St. John is coming. Let go my hands."

He dropped her hands and took a seat on the other side of the summerhouse, and a moment later St. John Ruthven presented himself at the doorway.

CHAPTER XVIII.

MEETING OF THE COUSINS.

St. John had come up the garden path quickly, and had failed to notice Harry Powell, although he had caught sight of a well-known dress which Marion wore.

Now, when he saw the young surgeon, his face fell, for he had calculated upon seeing Marion alone.

"Excuse me, Marion," he said, "I did not know you had company."

"Come in, St. John," replied the girl. "Do you not recognize my visitor? It is Dr. Harry Powell."

"Oh!" St. John was much surprised, and showed it. "How do you do?" he continued stiffly.

"Shake hands. You are cousins," went on Marion, not liking the dark look which had come to St. John's face.

"Excuse me, but I cannot shake hands with one who wears that uniform," returned the spendthrift, drawing back. "I am surprised, Marion, to see you upon such intimate terms with your country's foe."

Marion's face flushed, and she bit her lip. Harry Powell set his teeth and then smiled coldly.

"I perceive you wear no uniform at all, St. John," he remarked pointedly.

"No. My duty to my mother keeps me at home," stammered St. John.

"If all who have mothers were to remain at home we would have few soldiers."

"It is a very great trial to me to have to remain at home," went on the hypocrite smoothly. "Yet, to my notion, a man is far better off at home than to be wearing a Yankee uniform."

"That is for each man to decide for himself."

St. John turned to Marion.

"Does your mother know that Dr. Powell is here?"

"Yes; she has invited him to dine with us."

"To dine with you!" exclaimed the spendthrift.

"Yes, what is wrong about that?" questioned Harry Powell.

"I thought she was a true and loyal Southern woman."

"I do not follow you," answered Harry Powell hotly. "The ties of blood count for something, even in war times."

"They do not count for as much as that—to me," said St. John sourly.

"Then I presume you will not care to stop and dine with us, St. John," put in Marion.

"Thank you, no. I will remain another time—when it is more agreeable, Marion."

So speaking, St. John bowed low to the girl, nodded slightly to the young surgeon, and hurried from the place.

Marion looked at Harry Powell with a face that was crimson.

"Forget the insult, Harry!" she cried.

"It is not your fault, Marion. But what a cad St. John is! I never liked him much. I can easily understand how Jack cannot get along with him."

"I wish he would join the army. It might make a man of him."

"I believe he is too cowardly to don a uniform. But come, let us go into the house, or your mother will wonder what is keeping us."

When they entered the homestead they found Colonel Stanton taking his leave. The colonel was perfectly willing to allow the young surgeon to remain.

"Have a good time, Powell," he said. "And try to convince your worthy relatives that all Yankees are not the monsters they are painted."

"He's a downright good fellow!" cried Jack, when the Federal officer had departed. "I don't wonder that you like him, Harry."

"He is a very nice man," said Marion, and to this Mrs. Ruthven nodded affirmatively.

Dinner was almost ready to be served, and while they were waiting Marion noticed that the young surgeon was studying Jack's face closely.

"What makes you look at Jack so?" she questioned, in a low voice, so that our hero might not hear.

"I was studying his face," was the slow reply.

"Studying his face?"

"Yes. Marion, did you notice how Colonel Stanton looks?"

"I did, although not very closely."

"It seems to me that Jack bears a wonderful resemblance to the colonel."

"Now you speak of it, I must say you are right," answered Marion thoughtfully. And then, after another pause, she continued: "Is the colonel a married man?"

"I hardly think so. I have never heard him speak of a wife or children."

"Then it is likely that he is a bachelor." And there, for the time being, the subject was dropped.

Despite the fact that the house was surrounded by Federal troops and that a portion of the homestead was being used as a hospital, the dinner passed off in a far from unpleasant manner. Mrs. Ruthven was glad to meet her nephew once more, and made him tell the story of his service in detail. Not only the lady of the house, but also Marion and Jack, hung upon the young surgeon's words, and Jack's eyes glistened when he heard about the hard fighting which had been witnessed.

"Oh, how I wish I had been there! I would have helped to beat the Yankee troops back!" he cried.

"You're a born soldier, Jack!" answered Harry Powell. "And I must say I like you the better for it. I can't stand such stay-at-homes as St. John."

"Oh, St. John is a regular—a regular—"

"Hush, Jack!" interrupted Mrs. Ruthven reprovingly. "He says his mother needs him at home."

"And our country needs him at the front," said Marion.

"We don't need cowards," finished Jack. "Harry, you don't have cowards in your ranks, do you?"

"I am afraid all armies have more or less cowards in the ranks," laughed the young surgeon. "Some fellows would never make soldiers if they remained in the service a hundred years. Human nature is human nature the world over, you know."

"I wonder if Dr. Mackey is a brave man," muttered Jack, but nobody paid attention to this question.

The repast over, Harry Powell took his leave, but promised to come again, if possible, before leaving the vicinity. Marion saw him go with genuine regret, and blushed painfully when, on watching him hurry down the road, he suddenly turned and waved his hand toward her.

"Dear, good cousin Harry," she murmured. "How different from St. John!"

Two days passed and nothing of importance occurred to disturb the Ruthven homestead. On the second day St. John called to see Marion, but she excused herself by saying she had a headache, which was true, although the ache was not as severe as it might have been.

As he was leaving the place St. John ran up against Jack, who had been down to the outskirts of the Federal encampment, watching the soldiers drill.

"Hullo, where have you been?" said the spendthrift carelessly.

"Been down watching the Yankees drill," answered Jack.

"It seems to me you take an awful interest in those dirty Yankees," retorted St. John, with a sneer.

"I take an interest in all soldiers."

"Then why don't you join them, and evince your interest in some practical way?"

"I'd join our troops quick enough, if I was older. I'd be ashamed to stay at home and suck my thumb."

Jack looked at St. John steadily as he spoke, and this threw the spendthrift into a rage.

"Do you mean to insult me by that?" he roared.

"If the shoe fits you can wear it."

"I'll knock you down for the insult."

"I don't think you will."

"Why not?"

"Perhaps you are not able, that's why."

"Pooh! Do you think you can stand up against me?"

"Perhaps I can. Don't forget our encounter on the road."

"You took a mean advantage of me. I've a good mind to thrash you right here."

"You may try it on if you wish, St. John," and so speaking Jack began to throw off his coat.

"Will you take back what you said?"

"What did I say?"

"Said I was a coward for not becoming a soldier—or about the same thing."

"I won't take back what I think is true."

"So you dare to say I am a coward?" howled the spendthrift.

"If you want it in plain words, I do dare to say it, and furthermore, it is true, and you know it. Your plea that you must remain at home is all a sham. When the Yankees came this way you were all ready to run for your life at the first sign of real danger. You never thought of your mother at all."

"Ha! who told you that?"

"Never mind; I found it out, and that's enough."

"I—I was suffering from an extremely severe toothache, and hardly knew what I was doing that day."

"I don't believe it."

"You young rascal! you are growing more impudent every day."

"I am not a rascal."

"You are, and an upstart in the bargain. I heard at the village that some Confederate surgeon claims you as his son. Is that true?"

"If it is, it is his business and mine."

"Well, if you are his son, why don't you get out of here?"

"I shall not go as long as Mrs. Ruthven wishes me to remain."

"Does she want you to stay?"

"Yes."

"And Marion wants you to?"

"Yes."

"It is strange. But if I were you I wouldn't stay where I had no right to stay," went on St. John insinuatingly.

"But I have a right here."

"Indeed!"

"Yes. The late Colonel Ruthven adopted me, and I am his son by law."

"Bah! That will count for nothing if this Confederate surgeon can prove you belong to him."

"Well, he'll have to prove it first."

"Of course you won't get out of this nest until you are pushed out," blustered St. John. "It's too much of a soft thing for you. You ought to be made to earn your own living."

This remark made Jack's face grow crimson, and, striding up to St. John, he clenched his fists, at which the young man promptly retreated.

"I am perfectly willing to work whenever called upon to do so," said our hero. "But it is not for you to say what I shall do, remember that. I know why you wish to get me out of here."

"Do you, indeed!"

"I do, indeed, St. John Ruthven. You want to get hold of some of Mrs. Ruthven's property. If I was out of the way, you think she might leave it all to Marion and to you."

"Well, I have more of a right to it than you, if it comes to that."

"But Marion has the best right, and I hope every dollar of it goes to her."

"Well, that aint here or there. Are you going with your father or not?"

"He must prove that he is my father first."

"You won't take his word?"

"No."

"Why?"

"Because I do not like the man," and our hero's face filled with sudden bitterness. What if Dr. Mackey should prove to be his parent, after all? How St. John would rejoice in his discomfiture!

"I suppose this Dr. Mackey is a very common sort of man," continued the spendthrift, in an endeavor to add to our hero's misery.

"What do you know about him?"

"Nothing but what I heard at the village."

"Is he down there now?"

"Of course not. He went with our troops."

Jack drew a sigh of relief. It was likely that the doctor would not show himself in the neighborhood for some time to come, probably not until the Federal troops had departed.

"I am going to talk to my aunt of this," said St. John suddenly, and, without another word to Jack, turned his steps toward the plantation home.

CHAPTER XIX.

A SUMMONS FROM THE FRONT.

St. John found his aunt too busy to spend much time talking about Jack's past and Dr. Mackey's claim, and it was not long before he took his departure, feeling that he had gained nothing by this new attack upon our hero's welfare.

"I wish I could get him out of the way," he muttered, as he walked homeward, by a side road, so as to steer clear of the Federal troops. "If only he would join the army, and get shot down."

He entered his home filled with thoughts of Jack and Marion, but all these thoughts were driven to the winds after he had read a communication which had been left for him during his absence.

The communication was one from a well-known Southern leader of the neighborhood, and ran, in part, as follows:

"Many of us think it time to call upon you to take up arms as we have done. With our noble country suffering from the invasion of the enemy, every loyal Southerner is needed at the front. Join our ranks ere it be too late. The muster roll can be signed at Wingate's Hotel, any time to-day or to-night. Do not delay."

As St. John read this communication his face grew ashen. "Called upon to join at last!" he muttered. "What shall I do now? What excuse can I offer for hanging back?"

"What is in your letter, St. John?" asked his mother.

"They want me to join the army—they say every man is needed," he answered, with half a groan.

"To join? When?"

"At once."

"What shall you do?"

"I—I don't know." His legs began to tremble, and he sank heavily on a chair. "I—I am too sick to join the army, mother," he went on, half pleadingly.

Now Mrs. Ruthven did not care to have him leave her, yet she was but human, and it filled her with disgust to have her only offspring such a coward.

"You weren't very sick this morning."

"I know that. But the sun has affected my head. I feel very faint."

"If you don't join the ranks, all of our neighbors will put you down as a coward, St. John."

"They can't want a sick man along," he whined.

"They will say you are shamming."

"But I am not shamming. I feel bad enough to take to my bed this minute."

"Then you had better do it," answered Mrs. Ruthven, with, however, but little sympathy in her voice.

"I will go to bed at once."

"You must not forget that your cousin, Harry Powell, is in the army."

"Yes, on the Yankee side."

"Still he is brave enough to go. Marion may think a good deal of him on that account."

"Well, I would go, for Marion's sake, if I felt at all well," groaned St. John. "But I am in for a regular spell of sickness, I feel certain of it."

"Then go to bed."

"Write Colonel Raymond a note stating that I am in bed, and tell him I would join the ranks if I possibly could," groaned St. John, and then dragged himself upstairs and retired. Here he called for a negro servant and had a man go for a doctor.

Much disgusted, Mrs. Mary Ruthven penned the note, and sent it to town, shielding her son's true character as much as possible.

For the remainder of the day St. John stayed in bed, and whenever a servant came into his room he would groan dismally.

When the doctor arrived he was alarmed, until he made an examination.

"He is shamming," thought the family physician. But as the Ruthvens were among his best customers, he said nothing on this point. He left St. John some soothing medicine and a tonic, and said he would call again the next day.

Instead of using the medicine, the young spendthrift threw it out of the window.

"Don't catch me swallowing that stuff," he chuckled to himself. "I am not altogether such a fool."

Several days passed, and nothing of importance happened to disturb those at either of the Ruthven plantations.

But a surprise was in store for Jack and those with whom he lived.

One of the wounded soldiers stopping at Mrs. Alice Ruthven's home was named George Walden. The poor fellow had been shot in the shoulder, a painful as well as a dangerous wound.

For several days he lay speechless, and during that time the Confederate surgeon and Mrs. Ruthven, as well as Marion, did all they could to ease his suffering.

One day George Walden began to speak to Marion.

"You are very good to me," he said. "You are in reality an angel of mercy."

"I am glad to be able to help you, and thus help the Southern cause," replied Marion. "But you must not speak too much. It may retard your recovery."

"I will not talk much. But you are so kind I must thank you. What is your name?"

"Marion Ruthven."

Then he told her his own, and said he had a sister at home, in Savannah, Ga., and asked Marion to write a letter for him, which she did willingly.

After that Marion and George Walden became quite intimate, and the soldier told much about himself and the battles through which he had passed.

"Some of them are nothing but nightmares," he said. "I never wish to see the like of them again."

"And yet you saw only the fighting, I presume," said Marion. "Think of what those in the hospital corps must behold."

"I was attached to the hospital corps," returned George Walden. "I have helped to carry in hundreds who were wounded."

"If you were in the hospital service, did you ever meet a doctor named Mackey?" questioned Marion, with increased interest.

At this question the brow of the wounded soldier darkened, and he shifted uneasily upon his couch.

"Yes, I know Dr. Mackey well," he said, at last.

"You do!" cried the girl. "And what do you know of him? I would like to know very much."

"Is he your friend?" asked George Walden cautiously.

"No, I cannot say that he is."

"Because, if he is your friend, I would rather not say anything further, Miss Ruthven. I do not wish to hurt your feelings."

"Which means that what you have to say would be of no credit to Dr. Mackey?"

"Exactly."

"I would like to know all about him. I will tell you why. You have noticed Jack, my brother?"

"The lad who helped move me yesterday?"

"Yes."

"Of course—a fine young fellow."

"He is not my real brother. My parents adopted him about ten years ago."

"Indeed."

"Some time ago Dr. Mackey turned up here and claimed Jack as his son."

"Impossible! Why, Dr. Mackey is a bachelor!"

"You are sure of this? He says he was married to Jack's mother, who was shipwrecked on our shore, and who died at this house a few days later."

"I have heard Dr. Mackey declare several times that he was heart-free, that he had never cared for any woman, and consequently had never married."

At this declaration Marion's face lit up.

"I knew it! I knew it!" she cried. "I must tell mamma and Jack at once!"

"Dr. Mackey is a fraud," went on the wounded soldier. "To the best of my knowledge, he comes from Philadelphia, where he used to run a mail-order medical bureau of some sort—something which the Post-office Department stopped as a swindle."

"My cousin thought he came from Philadelphia," said Marion. "But wait until I call my mother and Jack."

Marion ran off without delay, but failed to find either Mrs. Ruthven or our hero, both having gone to town to purchase something at Mr. Blackwood's store.

"Da will be back afore supper time, Miss Marion," said one of the servants, and with this she had to be content.

"My folks have gone away," she said to George Walden. "As soon as they come back I will bring them to you. I hope you can prove your words."

"I am sure I can prove them," answered the wounded soldier.

"Jack does not like this Dr. Mackey in the least, and the idea of being compelled to recognize the man as his father is very repulsive to him."

"I don't blame the boy. For myself, I hate the doctor—he is so rough to the wounded placed in his care. He treated one of my chums worse than a dog, and I came pretty close to having it out with him in consequence."

"He doesn't look like a very tender-hearted man."

"He doesn't know what tenderness is, Miss Ruthven. I would pity your brother if he had to place himself under Dr. Mackey's care."

"We won't give Jack up unless the courts make us. My mother is firm on that point."

"But why does he want the boy?"

"That is the mystery—if Jack is not really his son."

"Perhaps there is a fortune coming to your brother, and the doctor wants to secure it. A man like Dr. Mackey wouldn't do a thing of this sort without an object. I can tell you one thing—the fellow worships money."

"What makes you think that?"

"Because I know that a wounded soldier once told him to be careful and he would give him all the money he had—twelve dollars. The doctor was careful, and took every dollar that was offered."

"But had he a right to take the soldier's money?" asked Marion indignantly.

"Not exactly, but in war times many queer things happen that are never told of at headquarters," answered George Walden.

Here the conversation ceased, for the soldier was quite exhausted. Soon Marion gave him a quieting draught, and then George Walden slept.

CHAPTER XX.

THE STORM OF BATTLE AGAIN.

As related in the last chapter, Mrs. Ruthven and Jack had gone to Oldville to do some necessary trading.

Arriving at the town, they found all in high excitement. The stores were closed, and only the tavern was open, and here were congregated a number of men who had but lately joined the Confederate ranks.

"What is the matter?" asked Mrs. Ruthven of one of the men.

"Another battle is on," was the answer. "We are going to drive the Yanks out of this neighborhood."

"Another battle!" cried Jack. "Where?"

"They are fighting over near Larson's Corners. Can't you hear the shooting?"

"I can hear it now—I didn't hear it before."

"Do you think they will come this way?" questioned Mrs. Ruthven anxiously.

"Aint no telling how matters will turn," answered the man addressed, and then hurried off to join the other newly enlisted soldiers. Soon the soldiers were leaving the town on the double-quick.

Jack watched the departure of the men with interest, and then espied Darcy Gilbert running toward him.

"Hi, Darcy!" he called out. "Where bound?"

"Jack! Just the one I wanted to meet. There's a fight on."

"So I hear. I reckon we had better call out the Home Guard again."

"By all means. The stores want protection, and so do the homesteads," went on Darcy. "Shall I go down the shore road and call up the boys?"

"Yes, and I'll take the Batsford road. If you see Doc Nivers tell him to call up the boys on the mountain road, will you?"

"Yes. What of those at Brackett's plantation?"

"I'll send Hackett or Purroy after them," answered Jack.

The two lads separated, and Jack turned to his foster mother.

"Mother, you heard what was said," he began. "You don't object, do you?"

"No, Jack; do your duty, as a brave boy should. But be careful—I cannot afford to lose you!" and she wiped away the tears which gathered in her eyes.

"You will return home?"

"At once."

"If I were you I'd place Old Ben on guard at the plantation. I don't believe anybody will harm the place, now it is flying a hospital flag. Certainly the troops under Colonel Stanton won't trouble us."

"No; he is a gentleman, and I know I can trust him. Dear Harry! I wish he was not with the Yankee army."

"Well, he is fighting according to the dictates of his conscience, so there is no use in finding fault."

Mrs. Ruthven kissed Jack tenderly and hurried off, and then with all speed our hero set to work to summon together the lads composing the Home Guard.

The task was not difficult, for the firing in the distance—which was gradually coming closer—had aroused everybody. In less than an hour the Home Guard was out in force on the town green, with Jack in command.

"Boys, we may have some hot work to do," said the young captain. "I expect everybody to do his best. I trust there is no coward among us."

"Not a bit of it!" came back in a shout.

"We aint no St. John Ruthvens," whispered one of the young soldiers, but loud enough for a dozen or more to hear.

"That's so," answered another. And then he continued, "What a difference between our Jack and his cowardly cousin!"

"We are here to defend property more than to take part in any battle," said Jack. "Do not let the guerrillas steal, no matter what side they pretend to be on. A thief is a thief, whether he says he is a Confederate or a Yankee."

"That's right!" shouted the old storekeeper, who stood by.

A little while later the firing came closer, and presently up the road a cloud of dust was seen.

"The Yanks are coming!" was the cry, as a horseman dashed up.

"Coming?" repeated several.

"Yes, they are in retreat!"

A wild shout went up—cut short by the sudden belching forth of cannon on the mountain side above the town. A little later some Federal troops swept into view.

"They are coming! Get out of the way!"

Soon the soldiers filled the road and the whole of the green. They had been fighting hard and were almost exhausted. Others followed until the streets of the old town were crowded. Then began a systematic retreat northward.

"We've got the Yanks on the run!" was the cry. "Give it to 'em, boys!"

The rattle of musketry was incessant, and ever and anon came the dull booming of cannon. Soon more Federal troops appeared, and those who had come first moved toward the mountain road.

It was a thrilling scene, and Jack longed to take part. But he realized that just now there was nothing for the Home Guard to do. Had they opened fire, the Federal troops would have annihilated them. Nobody molested the stores or town buildings, although the church was hit by several cannon balls. Gradually the fighting shifted to the mountain side, and then in the direction of the Ruthven plantations.

"They are moving toward St. John's place," remarked Jack, some time later, to Darcy. "We ought to go over to see that no damage is done there."

"St. John ought to take care of the place himself," grumbled Darcy. "He won't join the army or the Home Guard. What does he expect?"

Several sided with Darcy, but Jack shook his head. "I am going over. I would like eight or ten to go with me. The others had better remain around town." And so it was arranged.

The coming of the Federalists to the plantation owned by Mrs. Mary Ruthven filled St. John with supreme terror. Hearing the firing, the young man got up and dressed himself. He was just finishing when his mother appeared.

"St. John, Pompey says the Yankees are coming!" said the mother. "You must arm yourself and try to defend our home."

"The Yan—Yankees!" he said, with chattering teeth. "How—how near are they?"

"They have passed through the town and are all over the mountain side. Come, do not delay. I have given Pompey a gun and old Louis a pistol. Arm yourself and take charge of them. If we do not protect ourselves, we may all be killed."

Shaking so that he could scarcely walk, St. John went below and into the library, where hung a rifle over the chimney piece and also a brace of swords. He got down the rifle and loaded it. Then he strapped the larger of the swords around his waist.

"Now you look quite like a soldier," said his mother encouragingly. "I hope you can shoot straight."

"I—I don't want to kill—kill anybody," he answered. "If I do, the Yankees will be very—very vindictive."

"But you must protect our home!" insisted Mrs. Mary

Ruthven. "Come, brace up!"

Still trembling, and with a face as white as chalk, St. John walked to the veranda of the homestead. He gazed down the road and saw a body of soldiers approaching, in a cloud of dust and smoke. Then a cannon boomed out, and a ball hit the corner of the house, sending a shower of splinters in all directions.

"They have struck the house!" shrieked Mrs. Ruthven. "We shall all be murdered!"

"Spare us! spare us!" gasped St. John, as a company of soldiers came up to the mansion on the double-quick. "We have harmed nobody! Spare us!"

"You big calf!" cried one of the soldiers. "We aint going to hurt you. Git up from yer knees!" For St. John had indeed fallen upon his knees in his abject terror.

"Who—who are you?"

"We are Confederates—if you'll only open yer eyes to see. Git up!" And in disgust the Southern soldier pricked St. John's shoulder with his bayonet. The spendthrift let out a yell of fear, rolled over, and dashed into the house, leaving his gun behind him.

"St. John, where are you going?" cried his mother, coming after him.

"Oh, mother, we are lost!" he wailed.

"No, we are not. Go out again, and pick up your gun."

"I—I cannot! They will—will shoot me!" he shivered.

"But they are our own men, St. John. You are perfectly safe with them."

But he would not go, and she left him in the hallway, where he had sunk down on a bench. In one way he was to be pitied, for his fear was beyond his control.

Soon the Confederates left the plantation and the Federalists burst into view. The cannon continued to boom forth, and presently came a cry from the rear of the mansion:

"Fire! fire! The house is on fire!"

The report was true, and as the soldiers left the place up went a large cloud of smoke, followed by the bursting out of flames in several directions. Such was the state of affairs when Jack and his followers reached the roadway in front of the plantation.

"The house is on fire!" ejaculated the young captain. "Come, we must put out the flames."

"But the enemy—" began one of the other boys.

"The Yankees are making for the mountain road and our troops are to the westward. I don't believe either will come this way again. Hurry up, or it will be too late!"

Jack ran up to the house with all speed, to meet Mrs. Mary Ruthven on the veranda.

"The house—it is doomed!" wailed the lady of the plantation.

"Get us all the pails and buckets you have," answered Jack. "And have you a ladder handy?"

"There is a ladder in the stable, Jack. Oh, will you help put it out?"

"We'll do our best. Is St. John at home?"

"Yes," and so speaking, Mrs. Mary Ruthven ran off to arouse her son.

"You must help," she said. "Quick, or we will be homeless."

"But the—the Yankees?" he asked.

"Are gone." She clasped her hands entreatingly. "Oh, St. John, do be a man for once!"

"A man? What do you mean, mother?" he cried, leaping up as soon as he heard that the enemy was gone. "I am not afraid. I—I had a sudden attack of pain around my—my heart, that's all."

"Then, if it is over, save the house," she answered coldly, and ran off to tell the servants about the pails and buckets.

CHAPTER XXI.

A LIVELY FIRE.

In the meantime Jack and several others of the Home Guard had made their way to the barn and brought forth two ladders, a short affair and one which was both long and heavy.

"The short one can be placed on the veranda roof," said the young captain. "The other we can place against the corner, where the fire is burning the strongest."

"Somebody must have gone into the garret to set that fire," said another of the boys. "Where are the water buckets?"

"Here da am, sah," replied one of the negro servants, and handed them over.

"Somebody must keep at the well," said Jack. "Pompey, you know how to use the buckets best. You draw for us."

"Yes, Massah Jack."

"We'll form a line to the cistern, too," went on our hero. "Now then, work lively!"

The boys ran to the places assigned to them, and aided by the colored servants placed the ladders as desired. Soon water was being passed up and dashed upon the burning roof with all possible speed. But the fire was a lively one, and the breeze which was blowing helped it to spread.

"What can I do?" asked St. John, as he stood by, rubbing his hands nervously.

"Go down to the stable and the barns and put out the sparks blowing that way," said Jack.

"Don't you want me here?"

"Yes, if you'll go up to the top of the ladder," answered our hero, knowing full well St. John would do nothing of the sort.

"I—I never could climb a ladder," faltered the young man, and turned toward the stable, where he spent his time in putting out the flying sparks, as Jack had suggested.

It was hot work on the long ladder, and soon Jack was all but exhausted. But he stuck to his post, knowing full well that, if he let up, the fire would soon get the best of them. All of the boys worked like Trojans, and the negro servants helped them as much as possible. Mrs. Ruthven remained in the house, packing up her valuables, so as to be able to leave, should it become necessary to do so.

"More water!" cried Jack. "The fire is eating to the center of the roof! More water!"

"We are bringing it as fast as we can!" panted the boy below him.

"Make the servants form a line to the cistern."

"I will," answered the boy, and soon the water was coming up as rapidly as Jack and the other lad on the roof could handle it.

At last the fire seemed to lose its force, and was extinguished at one corner of the roof. Then all hands turned their attention to the spot over the veranda. Here the flames had eaten under the gutter.

"We must have an ax!" exclaimed Jack, and one was quickly procured from the woodpile.

"Hi! what are you going to do with that?" yelled St. John, as he caught sight of the article.

"Going to chop a hole in the roof," answered our hero.

"How foolish! You'll make the fire worse."

"No, I won't—I know what I am doing, St. John."

"You shan't chop a hole in the roof," insisted the unreasonable young man.

A cry of derision went up from half a dozen of the boys.

"Take a back seat, St. John," advised one. "You are too scared to know what you are saying."

At this the spendthrift's face grew as red as a beet.

"Shut your tongue, Larry Wilson," he retorted. "I say you shan't chop a hole in the roof. It will let the wind get to the flames."

"We want to get the water on the flames," replied Larry.

"And I say you shan't touch the roof with the ax!" screamed St. John. "I command you to stop."

"All right then, we'll stop," said Larry, and Jack said the same. In a moment more they were both on the ground, the other lads with them.

"Fo' de land sake, de house will burn up suah now!" groaned one of the negroes.

"If it does, it will be St. John's fault," answered our hero. He was thoroughly disgusted over the way St. John had acted.

"I'se gwine to tell de missus ob dis!" cried a second negro, and darted away in search of Mrs. Mary Ruthven.

Soon the lady of the house came running out, with a bundle in one hand and a box of jewelry in the other.

"What is this I hear, St. John?" she demanded.

"They want to chop in the roof, mother," he answered.

"We must make a hole, so that we can pour the water on the fire," explained Jack.

"Then go and make the hole," returned Mrs. Ruthven readily.

"And please be quick!"

"But, mother—" began St. John.

"St. John, they know more about putting out the fire than you do," was the tart reply of the young man's parent. "Let them do as they wish."

"All right then," growled the unreasonable son. "But if the house burns to the ground it will be their fault."

"It won't burn to the ground," answered Jack, and leaped up the ladder again.

Soon our hero was chopping away at a lively rate. In the meantime the others brought all the water possible to the scene.

When a hole was made in the roof the flames shot skyward for six or eight feet. At this St. John uttered a loud cry, almost of exultation:

"There, what did I tell you? Now the house will be burnt to the ground sure!"

"Lively with that water!" shouted Jack, ignoring him completely. And as the pails and buckets came up in a stream, he dashed the contents where they would do the most good.

It was perilous work, for the smoke rolled all around him, and more than once he was in danger of suffocation. But the water now did much good, and soon the flames began to go down.

"Hurrah! we have the fire under control!" shouted Larry.

It was true, and inside of quarter of an hour the last spark was put out. Then Jack crawled to the ground, almost too weak to stand.

"Is it out?" asked Mrs. Ruthven anxiously.

"Yes," answered our hero.

"Oh, I am so glad!" and she caught Jack warmly by the hand. At heart she was a true woman, and could appreciate what our hero had done for her.

St. John stood by in silence, hardly knowing what to say. At last he shuffled into the house.

"The water has made an awful mess," he declared, later, to his mother. "They needn't have drowned out the whole house like this."

"Don't say another word, St. John," answered his mother severely. "I am thankful the fire is out, even if you are not." And then she turned away to direct the servants in clearing away the muss that had been made.

The tide of battle had swept off in the direction of Jack's home, and anxious to know how Marion and his foster mother were faring, our hero soon after left Mrs. Mary Ruthven's plantation, and with him went Larry Wilson and three others of the Guard.

From a distance came the constant cracking of rifles and the booming of cannon.

"Let us take the short cut," suggested Jack, as he pushed across the fields. "There can be no time to spare."

"It is hard to tell who is winning to-day," returned Larry. "At first I thought the Yankees were in retreat."

"So did I, Larry. Well, we'll know how matters stand by night."

As they came in sight of our hero's home a Federal battery dashed into sight, drawn by horses covered with foam. The battery was followed by a regiment of infantry.

"Colonel Stanton's regiment!" cried Jack.

"They are in retreat!" answered Larry. "Look! our soldiers are coming down the hill after them like mad!"

"There is Colonel Stanton on horseback," went on Jack, straining his eyes. "What a fine figure he cuts!"

"Ba, Jack! how can you say that of a Yankee? I have half a mind to shoot him."

As Larry spoke he raised his gun, but Jack pulled it down.

"Don't, Larry!"

"Why not? We are at war, and he is our enemy."

"I know, but—"

"But what? Are you too tender-hearted to be a real soldier?"

"It isn't that, Larry. Colonel Stanton is such a fine man—"

"Those Yankees killed Colonel Ruthven, don't forget that," went on Larry earnestly. "We ought to bring down every one of them—if we can."

"Perhaps, but I would like to see Colonel Stanton spared—I cannot tell why."

On swept the soldiers, and for the moment the Federals were hidden by the smoke of gun fire. Then, as they reappeared, Jack set up a cry, half of alarm.

"What is it?" queried Larry.

"Colonel Stanton is shot!"

"Shot? You are sure?"

"Yes. See, he has fallen over the neck of his horse and several soldiers are running toward him. How sad! I wonder if he is dead?"

"If he is, it but serves him right, Jack."

"Perhaps; but I hope he isn't dead," answered Jack, with a peculiar look in his anxious face. As the Federal colonel disappeared from view he gave something of a groan, he could not tell why.

CHAPTER XXII.

AFTER THE BATTLE.

The Federal battery had gained a hill behind the Ruthven plantation, and from this point began to fire rapidly at the advancing Confederates.

Shot and shell sped over the homestead, and the inmates were, consequently, much alarmed.

"We will do well if we escape this murderous fire," said Mrs. Alice Ruthven to Marion.

"I wish Jack was here," answered the girl. "Where can he be keeping himself?"

"He remained behind to protect the property in town."

The tide of battle grew fiercer, and presently, just as Marion had gone to the kitchen to get something for the invalid soldiers, a heavy shot passed through the sitting room of the house, tearing down the plaster of two walls and damaging much of the furniture.

Of course all in the mansion were much alarmed. The negroes, especially, were panic-stricken, and ran forth in all directions.

"We is gwine ter be murdered," shrieked one. "Da is gwine ter shoot us all ter pieces!"

"Marion, are you hurt?" came from Mrs. Ruthven, who was in the front hallway at the time.

"No, mother. Were you hit?"

"No, Marion."

"Where did the shot strike?"

"Through the sitting room, I believe."

Both ran to investigate, and in the sitting room a sight met their gaze calculated to stun the stoutest heart.

Plaster and splinters lay in all directions, and the wounded soldiers were crying for aid and for mercy, thinking the enemy close at hand.

Under a mass of wreckage on the floor lay George Walden, senseless, and with the blood flowing from a wound in his temple.

"Oh, Mr. Walden is hurt, mamma!" shrieked Marion, and ran to raise him up.

They carried the wounded soldier to another part of the house and laid him on a fresh cot. Then, while Marion cared for him, Mrs. Ruthven went back to aid the others. In the meantime

Old Ben was instructed to hoist the hospital flag to a higher point on the mansion.

The shot appeared to be about the last fired in that vicinity, and soon the shooting came from a distance, as Federals and Confederates withdrew in the direction of the mountains.

"Mother! Marion! are you safe?" It was the cry from Jack as he came up, almost out of breath from running.

"Yes, thank Heaven, we are safe so far," answered Mrs. Ruthven. "Where have you been—at the town?"

"No, I was over to St. John's place," answered our hero, and in a few words told about the fire.

"We, too, have suffered," said Mrs. Ruthven. "A solid shot passed through the sitting room."

"Did it hurt anybody?"

"One of the wounded soldiers was knocked senseless. The others were more frightened than hurt."

"It has been a hot fight all around. And, oh, mother! what do you think? I saw Colonel Stanton shot down!"

"Is that true, Jack?"

"Yes, I saw the whole thing as plain as day. It's too bad. He was such a nice gentleman, even if he was a Yankee."

"You are right. Jack; he was indeed a gentleman. I felt perfectly safe while he was in the vicinity."

It was not long before Jack went upstairs to see how Marion was faring. He found his sister working over George Walden, trying to restore the hurt soldier to his senses.

"He is pretty badly off," said Marion. "I wish we had a doctor."

"Where is that surgeon who was here?"

"Gone to the battlefield."

"I don't know of any doctor to get just now, Marion."

"Then we must do the best we can ourselves. And by the way, Jack, this soldier knows Dr. Mackey."

"What?"

"Yes, and he said that Dr. Mackey is more or less of a fraud, and never was married."

"Oh, Marion! if he could only prove that."

"He thinks he can. He told me that the doctor came from Philadelphia, and Cousin Harry told me the same thing."

"We must follow up this man's record. I am now certain he is not my father."

"The soldier thought that perhaps there was property coming to you, and that Dr. Mackey wanted to get hold of it."

"I don't think he'd be above such a scheme, Marion. I never liked his looks from the first time I met him, at the bridge."

"I know that, Jack."

There was no time to say more, for there was too much to do. Marion continued her work around the sick rooms, and Jack went out to see how matters were faring at the stable and the barns.

He had hardly gained the vicinity of the stable when he heard a commotion going on within. Old Ben and two of the Home Guard boys were having a fight with three guerrillas, who were bent upon stealing several horses.

"Let go dem hosses!" Jack heard Old Ben cry. "Dem is private prop'ty; don't yo' know dat?"

"Git out o' the way, nigger!" cried the leader of the guerrillas. "We want these hosses, an' we are bound to have 'em!"

"If you touch the horses I'll fire at you!" came from one of the Home Guard boys, but scarcely had he spoken when one of the guerrillas raised his pistol and fired on the lad, wounding him in the shoulder.

This cowardly action made Jack's blood boil, and not stopping to think twice, he raised the gun he carried and blazed away. His aim took the guerrilla in the breast, and he sank down seriously, though not mortally, wounded.

A yell went up from the other guerrillas, and they fired at random, but did no damage to anybody but Old Ben, who was shot through the left shoulder. Then the other boys fired, and the guerrillas who could do so took to their heels.

"Ben, are you badly hurt?" asked Jack, when the encounter was over.

"Not wery, Massah Jack," answered the faithful old colored man, and went to the house to bind up his wound.

In the meantime the guerrilla who had been shot lay on the floor, raving and cursing in a frightful manner.

"Stop your swearing, or we'll do nothing for you," said Jack sharply, and then the fellow became more reasonable. He begged to have a doctor care for his wounds.

"We have no doctor here, but we'll care for you as best we can," said our hero, and this was done, although the guerrilla was kept at the stable, on a bed of straw.

At nightfall the fighting came to an end, and all became quiet around the plantation. It had been more or less of a drawn battle, and it was expected that the contest would be renewed at daybreak.

"Are you going to bed, Jack?" asked Mrs. Ruthven, a little after ten o'clock.

"No, mother; I think it best that I remain on guard," he answered. "Some of those guerrillas may come back, you know."

"But you must be tired out."

"I am; but I reckon I can stay up during the night without falling asleep at my post," he said, smiling faintly.

"Do as you think best, Jack; you and Marion must be my mainstays now," and she kissed him affectionately.

Hour after hour of the night wore along and nothing of moment happened. Jack spent the most of the time around the house, but toward daybreak made the rounds of the stable and barns.

He found the guerrilla groaning dismally.

"Give me sum terbacker, will yer?" asked the man presently.

Not wishing to appear too unkind, Jack procured a twist of tobacco for him, which he began to chew savagely.

"I'm in a putty bad fix, I reckon," said the guerrilla, after chewing in silence for several minutes.

"If you are, you have only yourself to thank for it," returned Jack coldly.

"Oh, I aint complainin', sonny. It's the fortunes o' war—as them poets call it, I reckon."

"You might be in better business than stealing horses."

"So I might, sonny—an' then agin' I might do wuss—yes, a heap wuss. I was gwine ter turn them hosses over to the Confed'rate government—they need hoss-flesh."

"You were going to do nothing of the kind. You are not a soldier, you are a common thief."

"Now, don't be hard on me, sonny. I fit on the right side, I did," drawled the guerrilla anxiously.

"You fought only for your own good."

"Taint so, sonny; I fit fer the glorious Stars an' Bars. Wot are ye calkerlatin' ter do with me, sonny?"

"I don't know yet. I reckon you'll stay where you are for the present."

"That's so too—I can't move nohow. Hullo, who's thet?"

At this question Jack turned suddenly—to find himself confronted by Dr. Mackey and two soldiers in Confederate uniform!

CHAPTER XXIII.

DR. MACKEY'S BOLD MOVE.

It must be confessed that Jack was startled, for he had not heard the approach of the surgeon and his companions, who had come up noiselessly and on foot.

"Hullo, you here?" asked Dr. Mackey, as he gazed at Jack in some astonishment.

"What brings you here, Dr. Mackey?" demanded our hero.

"I am looking for the dead or wounded in this neighborhood," was the answer. "Whom have you here?"

"A guerrilla we shot down."

"Ha! who shot him?"

"I did. He was trying to steal our horses."

"Dr. Mackey, don't you know me?" came from the guerrilla.

"Pete Gendron!" muttered the surgeon. "I never expected to see you here."

"Nor did I calkerlate to see you, doc. But I'm mighty glad yer come. Ye kin git me out o' this fix."

As he spoke, the guerrilla eyed Dr. Mackey sharply. On more than one occasion he had been the doctor's tool, and now he thought it no more than fair that the medical man should stand by him.

"Evidently you know this guerrilla," said Jack slowly.

"I do," answered the doctor slowly. He hardly knew how to proceed.

"I aint no guerrilla, an' Dr. Mackey kin prove it," cried Pete Gendron. The coming of the medical man had raised his spirits wonderfully.

"You are a guerrilla."

"I aint. Dr. Mackey will prove my words. He's a friend o' mine. Aint ye, doc?"

There was a peculiar emphasis to the guerrilla's words which made the surgeon shift uneasily from one foot to the other.

"If I don't humor Gendron, he may expose me," thought the surgeon dismally. "He knows too much to be made an enemy of."

"Is he your friend?" asked Jack.

"Not exactly my friend, Jack, but I know him pretty well," answered Dr. Mackey slowly, as if trying to feel his way.

"I aint a guerrilla, am I?" put in Pete Gendron eagerly.

"N—no, he is not a—a guerrilla," stammered the surgeon.

"There must be some mistake."

"I want to be taken to the Confed'rate hospital," went on Pete Gendron.

"But he and his comrades were trying to steal our horses," said Jack firmly.

"As I said before, my dear Jack, there must be some mistake," returned the surgeon smoothly. Suddenly his face brightened. "Gendron, you made a mistake by leaving the hospital so soon. Your fighting in to-day's battle must have made you light-headed. You probably came here by mistake."

The guerrilla was crafty enough to seize upon the cue thus given.

"Thet must be the size on it," he murmured. "My head has felt queer ever since I got out in the sun. Reckon I aint accountable fer all my actions, doc."

"He is a perfectly honest man," said Dr. Mackey to Jack. "I have seen him fight most bravely in half a dozen battles."

Jack felt that the surgeon was falsifying, but how could he prove it? Then he felt that there would be no use in keeping the guerrilla at the plantation.

"Well, take him away, if you want to," he answered. "But I shall still hold my opinion of the rascal."

"You are as insulting as ever, Jack," sneered the medical man. "I came here, hoping to find you of a different turn of mind."

"I shall never change my mind regarding you, Dr. Mackey," was our hero's ready reply.

"Come outside, I would like to talk to you in private."

The surgeon spoke in a whisper, and feeling there would be no harm in listening to what he might have to say, Jack followed him into the open.

"I want to know what you intend to do about coming with me, Jack," said the medical man, when they were out of hearing distance of the others.

"I don't intend to go with you, Dr. Mackey."

"You are hard on your father."

"Once and for the last time, let me say that I do not acknowledge you as my father."

"Nevertheless, I am your parent, and will soon be in a position to prove my claim."

"And when that time comes I may be in a position to prove you an impostor, Dr. Mackey."

"What! This to me!" ejaculated the medical man, in a rage.

"Yes, that to you."

"Boy, you are—are mad—you do not know what you are saying."

"I know perfectly well what I am saying."

"Prove me an impostor?"

"Yes."

"But how can you, when I am exactly what I claim to be."

"Dr. Mackey, where were you located before the war broke out?"

"You heard my story, Jack. There is no use to repeat it."

"You came from Philadelphia."

"Ha! who told you that?"

"You were connected with a medical company there which was put out of business by the post office authorities because of using the mails fraudulently."

At this assertion Dr. Mackey fell back as if shot.

"Jack, I demand to know who has told you this?"

"You are a bachelor, and were never married to my mother or to any other lady."

"I demand to know who told you this—this—string of falsehoods!" cried the doctor, catching our hero by the arm.

"A part of the story came from Mrs. Ruthven's nephew."

"What, St. John Ruthven? I hardly know the fellow."

"No, another nephew, Dr. Harry Powell, who is now attached to the Yankee army. He hails from Philadelphia."

"That viper!" ejaculated the medical man, then tried to check himself. "I—er—that is, I know Powell distantly. But he is much mistaken."

"I don't think so—and neither does Mrs. Ruthven nor Marion."

"So you have been harboring a Yankee in this place, eh? A pretty business to be in surely," sneered the surgeon.

"We could not help ourselves. But I have another witness against you."

"Another?"

"Yes, a Confederate soldier who knows you well. He can testify that you never had either sweetheart or wife."

"Who is the man?"

"For the present I must decline to disclose his identity."

"You are trying to fool me!" stormed Dr. Mackey.

"No, I am telling you only the truth. Now I wish you to answer me a few questions. Why are you so anxious to claim me as your son?"

"Because you are my son. Good or bad, I cannot go back upon

my own flesh and blood, as you are trying to do."

"I will never believe I am your son!" cried Jack impetuously. "Do you know what I think? I think you are trying to get hold of me so that you can obtain some money belonging to me."

"You—you little rascal!" cried Dr. Mackey. "How dare you talk to me in this fashion?"

"Because I believe you are a fraud, that's why," answered our hero defiantly.

A commingled look of rage and disappointment came into the medical man's face, which suddenly gave place to a look of cunning.

"I will make you smart for this," he stormed, and caught Jack firmly by both arms. "Garder! Mason! Come here!" he called loudly.

"What is wanted?" asked one of the Confederate soldiers, as both came rushing from the stable.

"Conduct this young man to our camp, and see that he does not escape from you."

"You shan't take me from home!" ejaculated Jack. "Let me go!"

He struggled to release himself, but the two soldiers were powerful fellows, and soon made him their prisoner.

"You are making a mistake," puffed Jack. "Dr. Mackey is a first-class fraud."

"Dr. Mackey is all right," put in Gendron, the guerrilla.

"He must be held," said the surgeon. "I will be responsible for this arrest."

"At least let me see Mrs. Ruthven before I go."

"No, take him away at once," cried the surgeon quickly. "Then you can return for Gendron."

"Where shall we take him, doctor?" asked one of the privates.

"To the old red house up the river. You know the place?"

"Yes, sir."

No more was said, and a minute later Jack found himself being conducted across the plantation by a back way. He wanted to cry out, but one of the soldiers leveled his gun and commanded him to keep silent.

As soon as the party of three was gone Dr. Mackey entered into earnest conversation with Gendron, at the same time giving attention to the guerrilla's wound.

"Very well, Pete," he said, at the conclusion. "Stick by me and I'll stick by you."

"It's a whack," replied the wounded man.

"If anybody from the house comes here, tell them that Jack went off to get some Confederate ambulance corps to take you away."

"I will."

A few words in addition passed between the pair, and then Dr. Mackey left the stable.

He was anxious to have another talk with Mrs. Ruthven, but concluded that he must postpone the interview until later.

"I reckon I have done enough for one night," he said to himself grimly. "With that boy in my power, perhaps she and the others will sing a different tune. Anyway, I'll not let the lad out of my grasp until he promises to do exactly as I desire."

CHAPTER XXIV.

THE HUNT FOR JACK.

"Marion, where is Jack?" asked Mrs. Ruthven, in the morning.

"I do not know, mamma."

"When did you see him last?"

"Just before he started for the stable last night."

Mrs. Ruthven was very much worried, and with good cause, as my readers know. She sought out Old Ben, who had his shoulder bandaged.

"Ben, have you seen Jack?"

"No, missus, I aint."

"Is he around the stable or the barns?"

"Perhaps he is, missus. Ole Ben will go an' look, if yo' want it."

"Yes, Ben; I cannot imagine what has become of him."

Old Ben hurried off, and Mrs. Ruthven went upstairs to wait upon George Walden, who had now developed a raging fever.

"It is very odd what has become of Jack," said the lady of the plantation. "He never went off like this before."

It was fully half an hour before Old Ben came back. The colored man looked much worried.

"Can't find him nowhar, missus," he said. "An' dat dar guerrilla is gone, too."

"The man who was shot while trying to steal the horses?"

"Yes, missus."

"Then something must be wrong. Didn't you find any trace at all of Jack?"

"Not de slightest, missus. Old Ben looked eberywhar, too—'deed I did, missus."

"I do not doubt you, Ben. But this is terrible. Jack must be somewhere."

"Dat's so, too, missus."

"Were there any signs of violence about?" asked Marion. "Any—any blood, for example?"

"Some blood at de stable. Miss Marion. But I rackon dat was from de shootin' ob dat dar guerrilla."

Marion heaved a deep sigh, and Mrs. Ruthven shook her head slowly. Here was fresh trouble, more painful than any that had gone before.

"The guerrilla couldn't go off alone, could he?" asked Marion.

"Jack said he was quite seriously wounded, Marion. Still, the rascal may have been playing possum with Jack, and stolen off on the sly."

"If he was strong enough to do that, perhaps he took Jack with him to keep the boy from sounding an alarm."

"You may be right. We must find the boy if we can."

Slowly the day wore away, and no tidings came to the plantation. Toward evening St. John put in an appearance.

"The soldiers have cleared out," he said. "There isn't a regiment of any sort within a dozen miles."

"I am glad of it," answered Mrs. Ruthven, and then continued quickly, "Have you seen anything of Jack?"

"Do you mean to-day?"

"Yes."

"No, I haven't seen him since he made such a mess of it up at our house, putting out the fire," growled the spendthrift.

"It's a wonder you didn't put out the fire yourself," put in Marion sharply. She did not like talk against her brother.

"I—I was sick, sicker than anybody supposed," stammered St. John. "Had I been at all well, things would have gone on very differently, I can assure you."

"Then you haven't seen or heard of Jack," said Mrs. Ruthven. "He has been missing since last night."

"No, I haven't seen him—and I don't want to see him. He insulted me and made trouble between me and my mother."

"On account of the fire?"

"Yes. He thinks he is a regular lord of creation, he does," went on St. John hotly. "He wants dressing down, Aunt Alice."

"I cannot believe Jack has done anything very wrong."

"He is a nobody, and puts on altogether too many airs."

Mrs. Ruthven would not listen to this talk, and changed the subject by asking him what had brought him over from his home.

"I was asked to come over and see if you had any of the Yankee wounded here."

"Who sent you?"

"Colonel Bromley of our army."

"No, we have only Confederates here."

"How many?"

"Five. Four of them are doing very well, you can tell the colonel, but the fifth was hurt when our house was struck by a cannon ball, and he is now in a high fever."

"All right, I'll tell him."

"Have you joined the army at last?" questioned Marion curiously.

"Not exactly, but I told the colonel I would help him in any manner that I could," answered St. John, and hurried away for fear of being questioned further.

The truth of the matter was that the fire had brought on a bitter quarrel between St. John and his mother, and the parent had insisted that the son overcome his cowardice and do something for his country. St. John had demurred in vain, and had at last gone to the Confederate headquarters and offered his services; but as a civilian, not as a soldier.

When the young man was gone Mrs. Ruthven and Marion had Old Ben and the others make another search for Jack, and this hunt lasted far into the night.

But it was of no avail; our hero had disappeared as utterly as if the earth had opened and swallowed him.

"Mamma, do you think it possible that the Yankees captured him?" was the question Marion put.

"Not unless Jack left home during the night, Marion. And what would cause him to leave without telling us that he was going?"

"That is true. Jack wouldn't do anything to cause us anxiety."

"It is a great mystery," sighed Mrs. Ruthven.

Later a negro, living on the mountain side, came down to the plantation and asked to see the lady of the house.

"I was t'inkin' yo' would be wantin' ter know wot became o' Master Jack," said the colored man, who rejoiced in the name of Columbus Washington.

"What do you know of him?" asked Mrs. Ruthven quickly.

"I seed him early dis mornin', missus—away up in the mountains."

"The mountains? Alone?"

"No, missus—he was a prisoner."

"Of the Yankees?"

"De men wot had him was dressed as Confed'rates, missus."

"You did not know them?"

"No, missus."

"And you are certain that Jack was held a prisoner?"

"Oh. yes, missus, fo' one ob de men said he would shoot if de boy tried to git away from him."

Mrs. Ruthven clasped her hands in despair.

"A prisoner! Did you speak to him?"

"No, no! I was afraid to show myself. De men was armed an' I wasn't—an' I didn't want to git in no trouble."

"Where were they taking Jack?"

"I can't say as to dat. I met dem on the ole mill trail near de blasted tree."

"You saw nobody else around?"

"No, missus."

"It is very strange why Jack should be carried off in this fashion. I wish you had followed them and seen what became of my boy."

"Perhaps I kin follow dem by de trail, missus. Ise putty good at dat."

"Then do so by all means, and I will reward you for your work."

"T'ank yo,' missus; yo' was always de lady to remember poor niggers."

"If you wish, you can take Old Ben with you. He is good at trailing, too."

So it was arranged, and half an hour later Old Ben and Columbus Washington were on their way. Both knew the mountains thoroughly, and lost no time in getting to the spot where Jack had last been seen.

Then began a hunt for the trail, and this discovered, both went on once more, little dreaming of the surprise in store for them.

CHAPTER XXV.

A REMARKABLE REVELATION.

Alarming news reached the Ruthven plantation that night. A large force of Federal soldiers had loomed up in the vicinity, and the Confederate army had been compelled to fall back to the mountains and to the valley beyond.

"Our victory is swallowed up in defeat," said Marion, but even as she spoke a soft look came into her eyes. Perhaps, if the Yankees were coming again, she would see Harry Powell once more. Even though she did not wish to acknowledge it to herself, Marion thought much of her dashing cousin.

"What a man he is, compared with cowardly St. John!" she said to herself. And then she prayed to Heaven that Harry might come out of the war unharmed.

Marion's wish was gratified so far as seeing Harry Powell was concerned, for the young surgeon dashed up on horseback early in the morning.

"I could not keep away," he said, after shaking hands with Mrs. Ruthven and his cousin. "I heard that the fight was fierce in this neighborhood, and I wanted to learn if you had suffered."

"We had a cannon ball go through the sitting room," answered Mrs. Ruthven.

"And was anybody hurt?"

"One of the wounded soldiers was hit. He has now a high fever in consequence."

"Thank God the cannon ball did not hit you or Marion!" ejaculated Harry Powell, and gave Marion a look that made the girl blush deeply. "Somebody said the Ruthven place had been on fire."

"That was at St. John's place," answered Marion. "But the fire was put out before great damage was done."

"I am happy to see that you were not hurt, Harry," said Mrs. Ruthven. "You must have been in peril many times."

"I was in peril, aunt, and I did not escape wholly. I was wounded in the shoulder, although the hurt is of small consequence."

"I am glad that you escaped," cried Marion. And she gave him a look that meant a good deal.

"Poor Colonel Stanton was not so fortunate," went on the young surgeon. "He was shot through the breast, and now lies between life and death."

"Jack saw him shot, from a distance," said Mrs. Ruthven.

"Did he? And where is Jack now?"

"He has disappeared," and the lady of the plantation gave her nephew some of the particulars.

Harry was invited into the house, and he remained to lunch, in the meantime telling of the general progress of the war.

"Frankly, I wish it was at an end," he said. "I hate to see one section of our glorious country fighting the other. It is not right."

During the talk it developed that Colonel Stanton was lying at a house about half a mile distant, up the bay road.

"He acts very queerly," said Harry Powell, "just as if his wound had affected his mind."

"Can we do anything for him?" asked Mrs. Ruthven.

"I do not know of anything now. But perhaps I'll think of something later, aunt. I do not wish the colonel to suffer any more than is necessary. He is a thorough gentleman."

"I feel you are right, Harry. He has given me an entirely different idea of Yankees from what I had before," returned Mrs. Ruthven warmly.

The lady of the plantation became deeply interested in the wounded colonel's case, and when the young surgeon went away she had one of the negroes of the place hitch up a horse to the carriage and drive her over to where the wounded officer lay.

The colonel was in something of a fever, and hardly recognized her. For a long time he kept muttering to himself, but she could not catch his words.

"The ship is doomed!" he cried suddenly. "We are going to pieces on the rocks!" And then he began to speak of the army and of the terrible battle through which he had gone.

"What can he mean by saying the ship is doomed?" was the question which Mrs. Ruthven asked herself. "Can it be that he was once in a shipwreck?"

For a long while after this the colonel lay silent. Then he opened his eyes and stared around wildly.

"All drowned, you say?" he exclaimed. "No! no! Laura must be saved! Save my wife—never mind me! How high the waves are running! Where is the child? Captain, why don't you put out to sea? Don't you see the rebels? They are luring us to the coast! See, that rebel is stealing my child, my darling Jack! Ha! we have struck, and I am drifting. Laura, where are you? Save Jack! Look, look, they are retreating! The battle is won! Oh, what a storm—can nothing be saved?" And then the poor man sank back, completely exhausted.

Mrs. Ruthven drank in the spoken words like one in a dream. What was this the wounded officer was saying? Something about a storm, about a wife Laura, and a child named Jack!

"Can it be possible that he is speaking of our boy Jack?" she asked herself, and then looked at the colonel's face more closely than ever. The resemblance was more than striking, it was perfect. Give Jack that heavy mustache and those wrinkles, and the faces would be exactly alike.

"He must be Jack's father!" she went on. "How wonderful! But what does this mean? Why did he not claim Jack long ago?"

For over an hour she sat by the colonel's side, but he made no further efforts to speak. In the meantime a surgeon came in to attend to the officer's wound.

"If you can have him taken to my house, I will see to it that he has the best of care," said Mrs. Ruthven.

"Why, are you not a Southern woman, madam?" questioned the surgeon, in pardonable surprise.

"I am, but I know Colonel Stanton, and do not wish to see him suffer any more than is necessary."

"He is a friend?"

"Something of a friend, yes."

"And who are you, if I may ask?"

"I am Mrs. Alice Ruthven, owner of the plantation half a mile from here. Dr. Harry Powell, whom you may know, is my nephew."

"I know Dr. Powell well, and if he says it is all right, I'll have Colonel Stanton removed to your home without delay."

"When will you see Dr. Powell?"

"To-day. This is not a nice place, and I would like to see the colonel have better quarters."

A little later Mrs. Ruthven left and drove home with all speed.

"Marion, I have wonderful news!" she exclaimed, on entering the room where the girl sat making bandages for the wounded soldiers.

"What is it, mamma; is Jack found?"

"No, but I am almost sure that I have found Jack's father?"

"Oh, mamma! Of course you don't mean that horrid Dr. Mackey?"

"No, I mean Colonel Stanton."

"Mamma!" And Marion leaped up, scattering the bandages in all directions.

"Did you ever notice how much Jack and the colonel resembled each other?"

"I did."

"The colonel is in a fever, and while I was there he cried out about a shipwreck, and asked that his wife Laura and his son Jack be saved."

"Didn't you always think Jack's mother was named Laura?"

"I did—although I wasn't sure."

"But why didn't he come to claim Jack?"

"That's the mystery. I have asked that the colonel be brought here, and as soon as he is well enough to stand being questioned I am going to learn the truth of the matter."

"I hope he is Jack's father," murmured Marion. "But if so, what of Dr. Mackey?"

"That's another mystery."

"He must know something of the colonel's past."

"Undoubtedly."

"I wonder if the two ever met in this vicinity?"

"There is no telling. I am impatient to question the colonel. But of course nothing can be done until he is better and in his right mind."

That evening there was the rattle of wagon-wheels on the gravel road leading up to the Ruthven mansion, and, looking out, Marion and her mother saw an ambulance approaching. The colonel was inside, and they hastened to prepare a bedroom for his accommodation.

"Is he better?" asked Mrs. Ruthven of the surgeon in charge.

"A trifle," was the answer. "What he needs is rest and quiet. He has a strong constitution, and that is in his favor."

It did not take long to transfer Colonel Stanton to the bedchamber prepared for his reception, and once he was in the house Mrs. Ruthven did all in her power to make him comfortable. The ride had somewhat exhausted the officer, and he slept heavily until far into the next morning.

CHAPTER XXVI.

DR. MACKEY SHOWS HIS HAND.

"Well, what do these fellows intend to do with me, anyway?"

It was Jack who asked himself the question, as he sat up, after quite a long sleep.

He was a close prisoner in a little cabin far up the mountain side. His hands were bound tightly behind him and were made fast to a heavy wooden stake driven into the hard mud flooring.

Night had come and gone, and all of the Confederates had left him. Now it was almost night again.

"If they would only give me something to eat and to drink," he went on. He was very dry, and his stomach was empty.

Half an hour later a footstep sounded outside, and Dr. Mackey appeared, carrying a knapsack filled with provisions, and a canteen of water.

"Sorry I had to keep you waiting. Jack," he said, as he set the articles down and proceeded to liberate our hero. "But I had the whole affair to smooth over, and I had also to get Gendron out of the muss," and he smiled grimly.

"Dr. Mackey, why do you treat me in this fashion?" demanded Jack.

"Because I want you to come to your senses and understand that I am your father."

"Do you think you are treating me as a father should?"

"A son who will not obey must be made to obey. Here, I have brought you something to eat and to drink. Fall to and make the most of it."

It would have been foolish to refuse the invitation, and our hero began to eat without delay. The surgeon watched him curiously.

"Jack, don't you think you are acting the part of a fool?" said the man presently.

"No, I do not."

"I offer you a name, a good home, and your share of a large fortune, and yet you turn your back on me and my offers."

"Have you a large fortune coming to me?"

"There is a large fortune coming to both of us. You shall have your full share of it—providing you will do as I wish."

"And what do you wish?"

"Well, in the first place, I wish you to let the world know that you are fully satisfied that I am your father."

"And after that?"

"After that I will resign my commission as a surgeon in the Confederate army and take the necessary steps to claim the fortune which awaits us."

"Why haven't you claimed the fortune before?"

"Because I had to prove that my wife had been drowned, and had also to prove that you were either alive or dead. Had you been dead, I could have taken the fortune for my own. But you are not dead, and so I am willing you shall have your share."

"Where is this fortune?"

"Never mind about that now. I will give you my word that, if all goes well, you shall have your full share."

"And how much will that be?"

"Not less than fifty or sixty thousand dollars. The whole fortune is worth over a hundred thousand dollars."

It must be confessed that our hero was staggered for a moment. The sum was certainly a large one—a good deal more than the Ruthven plantation was worth.

"It's a lot of money," he said, at last.

"Indeed it is, my boy. We can be happy on that amount for the rest of our lives."

"But you haven't proved to me that you are my father," went on Jack abruptly.

The crafty face of the surgeon fell, and he bit his lip.

"What more proof do you require?" he said coldly. "Do you suppose I would wish to divide that fortune with a stranger?"

"I presume not, nor would I wish to divide any fortune that was coming to me with a stranger."

"Ha! what do you mean?" gasped the medical man.

"I mean just this: That fortune may be coming to me, and you may be trying to gain possession of it by palming yourself off as my father."

The shot told, and Dr. Mackey staggered back and turned pale.

"Jack, you think you are smart, but you don't know what you are saying," he stormed.

"Perhaps I do, Dr. Mackey. One thing I do know—you are not to be trusted."

"What? This to my face?"

"You took the part of Gendron, when you knew he was nothing but a guerrilla and a horse-thief."

"I know nothing of the kind. Gendron has a good record

behind him. He was shot, and that may have hurt his brain."

"I don't believe that fairy tale. To my mind, you sided with him because you were afraid he would expose you."

"Boy, you are growing more bold. Don't you realize that you are in my power?"

"Am I?"

"Yes, you are—absolutely in my power. And you have got to do as I wish, or you'll take the consequences."

As Dr. Mackey spoke, he began to walk up and down the cabin nervously.

"What do you mean by my taking the consequences?"

"You'll find that out later."

"Would you kill me?"

"I would make you mind me—as a son should."

"I would rather do without the fortune than have you for a father, Dr. Mackey."

"Well, there is no love lost between us, when it comes to that, boy."

"Then you are willing to admit that you care more for the fortune than you do for me?"

"Why shouldn't I—after the way you have acted toward me? No father wishes a son who hates him."

"I will agree with you there," answered Jack slowly.

"If you don't wish to live with me, well and good—after we have our money. You can take your share and I'll take mine—and that will be the end of it."

"And you will let me return to the Ruthven plantation, if I wish?"

"Yes. But not until everything is settled."

"And what must I do to help settle it?"

"You must sign a paper acknowledging me as your father, and must bear witness to the fact of your being wrecked on this shore, and that your mother is dead. We will have to get Old Ben for another witness."

"And after that?"

"After that I will take the next step."

"You will not tell me more now?"

"No. I don't know whether I can trust you or not."

"But why this secrecy, if everything is aboveboard?"

"As I explained to Mrs. Ruthven, some distant relatives hold the fortune now, and if they learn of what I am doing they will at once take steps to head my claim off. I wish to spring a surprise on them."

"But if the claim is a just one, and half the property is coming to me, you do not suppose I am going to tell them in advance of what you intend to do."

"Boy, you do not understand such matters—you are not old enough," growled the surgeon. "Once more, and for the last time, will you do as I wish you to?"

"I will not promise yet."

"Then you shall remain here, a prisoner."

"For how long?"

"Until you come to your senses and agree to do as I wish."

A few words more passed, and then Dr. Mackey made our hero a prisoner again, and took up the canteen and the knapsack.

"You may have to remain alone for a long time," he said, on departing. "But if you get lonely and hungry, remember it is your own fault."

"I think you are a brute!" cried Jack after him. Then he listened and heard the surgeon's footsteps receding rapidly. Soon all became quiet.

Hour after hour went by, and nobody came near our hero. It was indeed lonely, and as the time passed his heart sank within him.

Then Jack heard the faint patter of footsteps over the dry leaves surrounding the cabin. The sounds came closer.

"Perhaps it's a dog," he thought. "I hope it is one from our plantation, on the hunt for me."

At last a shadow fell across the open cabin doorway and the figure of a strange creature came slowly into view. At the sight Jack could not suppress a scream. The visitor was a mountain wild cat!

CHAPTER XXVII.

COLONEL STANTON'S TALE.

Two days after being brought to the plantation Colonel Stanton's fever went down, and the surgeon who came to attend him pronounced the officer much better.

"But he must remain where he is for some time," said the medical man.

"He can remain as long as he pleases," declared Mrs. Ruthven. "I have no wish to hurry his departure."

She was anxious to learn the truth concerning the colonel's past, yet realized that she must move with caution, otherwise he might be thrown into another fever.

"Colonel Stanton," she said, seating herself at his side, "were you ever in the neighborhood before—I mean some ten or eleven years ago?"

At this question Colonel Stanton became immediately interested, and his wide-open eyes showed it.

"I do not know if I was in this neighborhood," he answered slowly.

"You do not know? Surely you must remember where you were at the time I mention."

"The time you speak about was a very bitter one to me, madam," was his slow answer.

"And you do not wish to speak about it?" she said softly, seeing the pain in his face.

"I have spoken to nobody about it for years, madam. Yet I would not mind speaking to you—you are so kind to me. During the time you mention I took an ocean voyage which was very disastrous to me and mine. The ship went down with all on board, including my wife and child."

"Did the ship go down on this coast?"

"She struck somewhere along the coast; where, I am not exactly sure."

"May I ask the name of the vessel?"

"She was the *Nautilus*."

Mrs. Ruthven's breast began to heave. "It must be true!" she murmured.

"What must be true, madam?"

"The *Nautilus* was wrecked on our coast here, not over half a mile from this plantation."

"You are sure of this?"

"I am. The wreck is still on the rocks in the bay."

"And were you living here at the time?"

"I was, and I know all about the wreck, and so does Old Ben, the negro who has the boathouse on the shore."

The wounded officer's interest increased.

"I would like to visit that wreck some time, if it is still intact," he said. "I left some valuable papers in a secret closet. It is possible they are still on board."

"Do you know who was saved from the wreck?"

"Saved? No one was saved."

"You are mistaken—a lady and her child were saved. The lady died two days later, but the child still lives."

"What was the name of that lady? Tell me, quick?" gasped the officer, and tried to sit up, but fell back through weakness.

"Do not excite yourself, Colonel Stanton, I beg of you!" pleaded Mrs. Ruthven, in alarm, fearful of the patient's agitation.

"But tell me the name of that lady—and was the child a boy?"

"I do not know the name of the lady, for she was badly hurt and could not give it. The boy's name was Jack."

"Jack! My child's name was Jack. And you say he still lives?"

"He does. The child is our Jack, for my husband and I adopted him."

"Your Jack? That fine, manly fellow? Oh, Mrs. Ruthven, send him to me at once!"

"I cannot do that just now, Colonel Stanton."

"If only we can prove he is my son! Have you nothing belonging to the lady?"

"Yes, I have her clothing, also the little boy's, and some jewelry."

"Bring them to me," and now the colonel sank back, too weak to say more.

As much agitated as her patient, Mrs. Ruthven hurried from the room, and presently returned with the clothing, the lace handkerchief, and the wedding ring.

"They were my darling Laura's!" murmured Colonel Stanton, as he gazed at the things. "And this was little Jack's dress. Mrs. Ruthven, beyond a doubt Jack is my son!"

"I suspected as much two days ago, Colonel Stanton. When you had a fever you spoke of a shipwreck and of the loss of your wife and son Jack. Yes, Jack must be your son. But how were you saved?"

"It is a strange tale, madam. As you know, my wife and my son were washed ashore. I thought them drowned. Hours after I found myself, I scarcely know how, clinging to a spar, tossing up and down on the dreary waste of waters, far out to sea."

"And you were picked up?"

"Not for twenty-four hours or more. Then those on a passing ship espied me, and sent out a small boat to my rescue. I can remember how they hauled me in, and how I shrieked with joy, and then fell to the deck unconscious."

"The exposure was too much for you."

"Yes, and it not only affected my body, but likewise my mind, for it is only in a dim, uncertain way that I remember being taken on a voyage of several weeks' duration, and then finding myself in a strange-looking hospital. There I remained for two months, and was then transferred to an insane asylum."

"An insane asylum! Colonel Stanton, how you must have suffered!" cried Mrs. Ruthven sympathetically.

"That was not the worst of it, madam. At the asylum I was treated most brutally by a good-for-nothing physician, who did his best to pry into my family affairs."

"And who was that physician, Colonel Stanton? Excuse my curiosity, but I have a strong motive for wanting to know."

"He was a tall, wicked-looking fellow, who went by the name of Mackenzie, although I have since learned that his real name is Mackwell or Mackey."

"Dr. Mackey! He has been here."

"Here?"

"Exactly, and he claims Jack as his son!"

"The vile impostor!" cried the wounded officer wrathfully. "He is a villain to his very finger tips. It is to him that I owe my long term in the insane asylum. Where is he now?"

"That I cannot tell you. I refused to give Jack up, for I did not like the looks of the man, and moreover Jack did not wish to go with him. I told him he would have to prove his claim at court."

"That was right. If I can get my hands on him, I will either shoot him or place him behind the bars."

"He certainly deserves arrest for plotting to take Jack."

"I presume he is scheming to obtain the property which is rightfully mine. During my lucid intervals at the asylum he got me to tell him my story. There was property in England coming to me, and also an estate in Virginia coming to my wife. The trip on the ocean was taken to obtain the property coming to Laura. He drew from me all the details he could, and then drugged me, so that for a long time I knew scarcely anything of what happened. When I regained my own mind, I learned that he had left the asylum several weeks before, and departed for parts unknown."

"And were you kept at the asylum?"

"I was, for years, for this rascal had put me on the books as being incurable, and subject to attacks of great violence."

"Of course he did this to obtain possession of the property."

"Undoubtedly."

"It is strange he did not put in an appearance before."

"You must remember he knew no more than I about the exact fate of the *Nautilus*. How he found out the vessel was wrecked here I do not know."

"He has paid the wreck a visit—Old Ben rowed him over to it!" cried Mrs. Ruthven, struck with a sudden idea.

"Did he bring anything away with him?"

"Old Ben thought he brought with him a tin box."

"It must have been my box—the one I placed in the secret closet! I must get it away from him. But tell me of Jack. When will he be back?"

"I—I cannot say, Colonel Stanton."

"Did you send him away on an errand?"

"I—I did not."

"But he is not here. Tell me, is he—is he missing—shot?"

"He is missing, yes. I do not believe he has been shot."

"It must be more of Dr. Mackey's work," muttered the wounded officer, and then sank down. The conversation had exhausted him utterly, and it was a long while before he spoke again.

CHAPTER XXVIII.

IN THE HANDS OF THE GUERRILLAS.

Our hero knew only too well how dangerous a wild cat can be, and as he gazed at the beast looking in through the open doorway of the lonely cabin his heart was filled with dread.

"A wild cat!" he muttered. "Scat! go away!" he yelled.

The sudden cry caused the beast to retreat a few steps, and for the instant Jack breathed easier. But then the beast approached once more.

"Go away! scat!" he repeated, but now the wild cat stood its ground, its eyes gleaming fiercely and its mouth half open, showing its sharp teeth. It was tremendously hungry, and this had caused it to find its way to the habitation.

"Go away, I say," repeated Jack, and then, as the wild cat took a noiseless step forward, he let out a scream: "Help! Help!"

The wild cat now prepared to leap upon him. It crouched low, shaking its short tail from side to side. The leap was about to be taken when, of a sudden, bang! went a gun, and the beast rolled over on its side.

"A good shot, Ben!" came in the voice of Columbus Washington. "I rackon ye killed him."

"Ben!" cried Jack, in great joy, as the face of the faithful old negro showed itself at the doorway. "You came in the nick of time!"

"Dat's so," answered Old Ben, as he came forward and poked the wild cat with his gun barrel. "Dead, are ye? Well, Old Ben will make suah," and he hit the wild cat's skull a blow that crushed it completely.

"Ben, you saved my life," went on Jack joyfully. "I was certain I was going to be chewed up."

"Wot fo' is yo' a prisoner yeah?" asked Columbus Washington, as he gazed at Jack's bonds curiously.

"Dr. Mackey made me a prisoner."

"What, dat man!" ejaculated Old Ben.

"Yes, Ben; he had me taken from the stable, where I had gone to watch that guerrilla."

"And where am de guerrilla?"

"Dr. Mackey helped him to escape."

The faithful old colored man shook his head doubtfully.

"Massah Jack, do yo' dun t'ink dat doctor am your fadder?"

he asked.

"No, Ben; I think nothing of the kind."

"Neider do I. He is a-plottin' against yo'."

"That is what I think, Ben. If I could manage it, I would have him arrested. Then we could get at the bottom of this affair."

Jack was speedily released, and the party of three left the lonely mountain cabin and started across the country for the Ruthven plantation.

"Yo' mudder will be tickled to see yo'," remarked Old Ben, as they trudged along. "She was worried to death ober yo' absence."

"After this I will see to it that they don't get me again," replied our hero.

Half a mile was covered when, on turning a point in the trail, they came unexpectedly upon a company of Confederate guerrillas who were taking it easy, lying in the grass.

"Hullo! who are you?" demanded one of the guerrillas as he leaped up and drew up his gun.

"Friends!" answered Jack.

Just then he caught sight of the men who had marched him away from the stable, and also of Pete Gendron, who was lying on some blankets in the shade.

"Friends, are you!" cried one of the men who had marched him off. "Up with your hands, sonny!"

There was no help for it, and Jack put up his hands, and his negro companions did likewise.

"I reckon as how we cotched ye nicely," went on the man with the gun. "Whar did ye come from—thet cabin up the mountain?"

"Yes."

"Whar is Dr. Mackey?"

"I do not know."

"Did he let ye go?"

"Of course he didn't let the boy go," growled Pete Gendron. "The niggers must have released him."

"Is that true, sonny?"

"That is none of your business," answered Jack, not knowing what else to say.

"Aint it, though? All right, ride yer high hoss, if yer want to. But throw down them arms fust."

"What do you mean?"

"I mean all of yer are prisoners, thet's wot I mean," drawled the guerrilla.

"You have no right to hold me up in this fashion."

"Ye forgit, sonny, thet might makes right in most cases. Come, hand over them firearms."

Jack had been provided with a pistol by Old Ben, and this he was compelled to surrender, and his companions were also disarmed. The guerrillas numbered fully a score, so resistance would have been foolhardy.

"What do you intend to do with me?" asked our hero, after he had been made a prisoner by having his hands bound behind him.

"We'll hold ye till Dr. Mackey comes back."

"When will that be?"

"Can't say."

This ended the talk, and presently the guerrillas moved up the mountain side to where there was a fair-sized cave.

They marched our hero into this cave, and tied him and his companions fast to some jagged rocks in the rear.

A fire was started up and the outlaws—for the guerrillas were nothing less—proceeded to make themselves comfortable by lying around, drinking, smoking, and playing cards.

Gendron was not badly wounded, and sat up to look on at the card-playing.

So the hours wore away. Toward night a scout went out to learn what the armies were doing, and he did not come back until the next day.

Two days were spent by Jack and his companions in the cave. During that time the guerrillas treated them brutally, and gave them hardly sufficient food to keep them from starving.

Gendron was particularly bitter against Jack, and insulted our hero upon every possible occasion.

"If I was the doctor I'd blow your head off, and get that money for myself," he said once.

"What do you know about that money?" demanded Jack.

At this the guerrilla closed one eye suggestively.

"I know a whole lot, sonny."

"Then you know what a rascal Dr. Mackey is?

"I didn't allow as how he is a rascal, sonny."

"Well, he is, and you know it. I can't see how he puts up with a fellow like you, though."

This was said to draw Gendron on, and it had the desired effect.

"He can't help himself," chuckled the guerrilla. "I know too much."

"What do you know."

"I know all about the doctor's private papers—the ones he carries in the tin box."

"The papers about the property?"

"O' course."

"Those papers won't help him any," went on Jack, wondering what the guerrilla would say next.

"Won't they? They'll prove that he is—. But never mind—you shan't git nothin' out o' me," and then Gendron relapsed into sudden silence, as though he realized that he had been talking too much.

On the afternoon of the next day Dr. Mackey appeared, accompanied by another man, evidently an officer of the guerrillas. His face grew dark as he gazed first at Jack and then at Old Ben and Columbus Washington.

"So you were going to help Jack to escape," he said harshly to the negroes.

"Jack is my young mastah," replied Old Ben. "Why shouldn't I try to sabe him?"

"You are the fellow who saved Jack years ago, when the shipwreck occurred, I believe."

"I am, sah."

"Then I am glad I have you in my power," answered Dr. Mackey. "You may prove useful to me."

CHAPTER XXIX.

THE ESCAPE FROM THE CAVE.

Dr. Mackey turned away to consult with the guerrillas, and Jack and his companions were left to themselves for the best part of half an hour.

The surgeon was evidently much disturbed over something, and Jack caught the words, "must leave the country," and "I will send the money," spoken to the guerrilla captain.

"Can it be possible that he intends to leave the States?" mused our hero. "Well, we can easily get along without him. But I would like to know more of that fortune."

At length Dr. Mackey came to him and sat down by his side.

"So you thought to escape me, did you?" he began.

"Do you blame me?" questioned our hero, as coolly as he could.

"Not exactly. But I want to warn you that it won't pay to try to escape again. I have given the soldiers orders to shoot you down, if you attempt it."

"In that case they must be outlaws, not soldiers, Dr. Mackey."

"They know how to obey orders."

"Again I demand to know what you are going to do with me."

"If you wish to know so much, I will tell you. I am going to take you out of the country."

"To where?"

"That you will learn after we are on shipboard."

"Then you intend to take me away from America?"

"Yes."

"Are you going to take me to Europe?"

"As I said before, you'll learn your destination when you are on shipboard."

"Supposing I won't go with you?"

"If you won't go peaceably, I'll have to use force, that's all."

"You mean you'll drug me, or something like that?"

"Never mind the details. You'll go with me, and that ends it. Moreover, you'll do just as I want you to."

"When do you intend to take me away?"

"That will depend upon circumstances. Probably to-morrow night, or the next day."

"What of my companions?"

"Old Ben shall go with us."

"And Columbus?"

"Is that the nigger's name?"

"Yes. Columbus Washington."

"The guerrillas will take care of him."

"Do you mean to say they will shoot him?"

"What if they do? Niggers don't count in this world."

"I think you are a monster, Dr. Mackey!" exclaimed our hero, in horror. "To kill a negro is as much murder as to kill anyone else."

"I won't discuss the subject. The question is, will you go along peacefully with me?"

"I will not. You have no right to abduct me in this fashion."

"I have a right to do as I please with my own son."

"Again I say I am not your son. Do you know what I think? I think you are nothing but a swindler—a rascal who wishes to use me as a tool, in order to get hold of some fortune coming to me or to somebody else."

Dr. Mackey glared at Jack for a moment, then leaped forward and struck our hero a cruel blow in the face.

"That for your impudence!" he cried wrathfully. "After this, keep a civil tongue in your head."

The blow made Jack's blood boil, but he was helpless to resent it. "You are a coward, to hit me when I am tied like this," he said. "But some day, Dr. Mackey, I may be able to square accounts, and then you had better beware."

One of the guerrillas now came forward to consult with the surgeon, and Jack was left with the other prisoners, to meditate over what had been said and done.

"He's de wust rascal wot I eber seen," whispered Old Ben sympathetically. "Wot a pity he wasn't shot down in de fust battle wot he eber got into!"

"He wants to take us both out of the country, Ben."

"Wot, away from ole South Carolina?"

"Yes—on a trip on the ocean."

"I don't want to go, Massah Jack."

"No more do I; but how can we help ourselves?"

"I wish dis niggah could git free, Massah Jack."

"We must try our best to escape to-night. If we don't do it to-night, I reckon our last chance will be gone."

"Ise willin' ter do all I kin," answered Old Ben, and the other negro said the same.

With the setting of the sun over the mountains a strong breeze sprang up, and presently the sky was obscured by heavy clouds.

Dr. Mackey had gone off half an hour before.

"We're in fer a heavy storm," Jack heard one of the guerrillas say. "It's a good thing we can crawl into the cave when it comes."

"If they come in here our chances of escape will be slim," thought our hero.

The approaching storm made it very dark in the cave, and during this time he worked with energy at his bonds.

At last he was free, and without making any noise he rolled over and released Old Ben and Columbus Washington.

Suddenly there was a shout from outside.

A guerrilla on guard had discovered a man on the trail, with two horses loaded with store goods.

"Here's a chance fer a haul!" was the cry.

The guerrillas ran outside, and soon the majority of them were making after the traveler.

Only two were left on guard, and one of these was more than half overcome by the liquor he had imbibed.

"Now is our chance!" whispered Jack, as he tiptoed his way to the cave entrance. "Ben, you and I will pounce upon that man with the gun. Columbus, you silence the fellow sitting on the rock. We must not let them cry for aid."

The negroes understood the plan, and in a moment more the party of three were upon the guerrillas. While Jack seized the gun of the one, Old Ben caught him from behind and placed a large hand over his mouth.

"Silence, on your life!" said Jack, and leveled the gun at the rascal's head. The man understood and, when allowed to breathe, said not a word.

To capture the half tipsy sentinel was likewise easy, and after both were disarmed they were ordered to enter the cave.

"If you make the least outcry we'll come back and shoot you," said Jack.

Then he motioned to the two negroes, and all three set off on a run down the mountain side. They heard a rifle shot to the right, and consequently moved to the left.

The storm now burst over the mountains in all of its fury, with vivid flashes of lightning and sharp cracks of thunder. As they proceeded they heard the distant falling of one tree or another, as the giants of the forest were laid low by the elements.

"I dun rackon da won't follow us in dis yeah storm," remarked Old Ben, as they stopped after a while, to catch their breath. "Da will be fo' gittin' back to de cabe an' stayin' dar."

"I hope that traveler escaped them," answered Jack. "But

those gun-shots sounded dubious."

"De gorillas ought all to be hung!" came from Columbus Washington. "Da aint no sodgers, no matter if da do w'ar a uniform."

"They are outlaws, pure and simple," answered Jack. "But come, we must go on. Ben, how far are we from home, do you calculate?"

"Six or seben miles, Massah Jack."

"Then we have a good, stiff walk before us."

"Do yo' t'ink yo' can walk dat far, Massah Jack, in dis awful storm?"

"I can, unless the rain sets in harder. I am anxious to get back, you know."

"I don't blame yo' fo' dat, Massah Jack. De folks will be mighty glad to see yo', too," answered Old Ben.

On they went through the darkness, Old Ben following the trail with the keenness of a sleuth-hound. But it was far from a pleasant journey, as Jack soon discovered, as he stumbled along over dirt and rocks and through the dripping bushes. He was soaked to the skin, and the rawness of the air caused him to shiver.

The downpour was now extra heavy, and they had to come to a halt under some trees, in order to get their breath again. The wind was blowing strongly and it was directly in their faces.

"How many miles have we made, Ben?" asked Jack.

"Not more dan t'ree, Massah Jack?"

"Then we have nearly four still to cover."

"Yes, Massah Jack, an' wery hard roads, too, ober Hallack's hill."

"If there was a cabin handy, I would go in for a rest of an hour or two. The storm may let up."

"Da is a cabin down de trail, on de bend."

"Then let us stop there."

So it was arranged, and soon they gained the cabin, which was deserted, the owner having joined the soldiers a year before, and his wife and children being with some relatives in the town.

It was easy to get into the cabin, and once inside they started to make themselves as comfortable as possible.

But they had not been in the place over half an hour when voices outside filled them with fresh alarm.

CHAPTER XXX.

BROUGHT TO BAY.

"Somebody is coming!" whispered Jack excitedly. "I wonder if it is the guerrillas?"

"If da come, de jig am up!" groaned Old Ben.

"Let us hide upstairs," returned our hero. "Quick!"

There was no time to say more, and all three ran for the ladder leading to the loft of the cabin, which was but a story and a half high. Jack was the first up, and the negroes quickly followed, and then all lay low on the flooring, hardly daring to breathe.

In a moment more two men entered the cabin, shaking the water from their rubber cloaks as they did so. The two men were Dr. Mackey and St. John Ruthven.

"What a beastly night!" exclaimed St. John with a shiver. "When I left home to meet you I never expected such a storm as this. If I had, I shouldn't have come."

"I didn't look for such a rain myself," returned Dr. Mackey, throwing off his cloak. "Anybody around?"

"Don't seem to be, although there are muddy footprints on the floor."

The two gazed around, but Jack and his companions were wise enough to keep out of sight, and apparently satisfied that the cabin was deserted, Dr. Mackey flung himself on a bench and St. John did likewise.

"You said you wished to see me on important business," observed the spendthrift.

"I do," was the reply. "I wish to help both you and myself."

"In what way."

"In several ways, Mr. Ruthven. In the first place, you are aware that I claim Jack as my son."

"I know that."

"I am very anxious to establish my claim to the boy."

"I don't see how I can help you, Dr. Mackey, although I am glad enough to have you claim Jack."

"You ought to help me, for it will be helping yourself as well. Your aunt thinks a great deal of Jack. If he is allowed to remain at the plantation she may take it into her head to leave him half of her property."

"I know that, too."

"The property ought to go to that girl and to you. With Jack out of the way you will be pretty certain of your share."

"But I don't understand your game, Dr. Mackey. Why do you want Jack, if he doesn't care for you?"

"I love the boy, in spite of his actions. Besides, he must come with me in order that I may establish our joint right to a fortune which awaits us."

"Well, what do you want me to do?" questioned St. John, after a pause, during which Jack waited with bated breath for what might follow.

"Jack was picked up from a shipwreck nearly eleven years ago. He and his mother were taken to your aunt's home, and it was from this home that Jack's mother, my wife, was buried."

"Well?"

"I am quite certain that your aunt is keeping all of the things which were taken from my wife's person at the time of her death, and also the clothing Jack wore when he was rescued. I wish to obtain possession of those things, or, failing that, I want to get a minute description of them."

"Do you want me to get the things for you?"

"If you can."

"But my aunt may object to giving them up."

At this the face of Dr. Mackey fell.

"I'm afraid you don't quite understand me, Mr. Ruthven. I don't want your aunt to know anything about it."

"Oh!" St. John's face became a study. "You—er—you wish me to get the things on the sly?"

"Yes. You must remember they belong to me. But if you tell Mrs. Ruthven she will be sure to raise a big fuss, and that is what I wish to avoid."

"I don't see how I can get the things?"

"Can't you get your aunt or your cousin to show them to you? Then you can watch where they are put, and the rest ought to be easy."

"I'm afraid my aunt is very careful of the things. I have heard her say as much, to my cousin Marion."

"Well, you ought to take a little risk. Remember, it is to your interest to help me in establishing my claim to Jack."

"I'll do what I can," replied St. John, after a moment's consideration.

"I would like to get the things as soon as possible."

"I'll go over to my aunt's plantation the first thing in the morning. But she may not want to listen to me just now. She is extra busy, you know."

"With those wounded Confederate soldiers?"

"Not only with those, but she also has a Federal officer there—brought in a few days ago."

"A Federal officer? Does she sympathize with the North?"

"She does to some extent."

"Who is the fellow?"

"A Colonel Stanton."

At the mention of that name Dr. Mackey leaped up in alarm.

"What! that man—in her house!" he gasped.

"Do you know Colonel Stanton?"

"I—that is—I know of him. Is he badly wounded?"

"I think he is."

"I hope he dies then. He is—a—a—very bad customer to meet."

"I can't understand why my aunt makes so much of him."

"Tell me, has this Colonel Stanton met Jack?"

"Yes, they met some time ago, when the Yankees first came to this neighborhood."

"Ah!" Dr. Mackey drew a long breath. "I wonder what Jack thought of the colonel?"

"He likes the Yankee very much."

"Humph! Well, there is no accounting for tastes." Dr. Mackey pulled himself together with an effort. "If you see this Colonel Stanton don't tell him about me, or repeat anything I have said, will you?"

"I don't want to see the Yankee. I haven't any use for any of them."

"Colonel Stanton ought to be arrested as a spy. I know for a fact that he once entered our lines and reported our movements to his superiors. It would be a feather in your cap if you could have him arrested by the Confederate authorities."

"By Jove! do you really think that?" asked St. John, with renewed interest.

"I do."

"Then I'll report the case without delay. I thought he was something of a sneak the first time I saw him."

"If the South would hang him as a spy it would be a good job done."

"Would you be willing to appear against him?" asked St. John anxiously.

"Well—er—no, but I can bring two other men to appear."

"Then I'll surely have him arrested."

"And what about those things?"

"I will get them, if I possibly can."

A loud clap of thunder interrupted the conversation at this point, and when it was renewed the topic was not of special interest to Jack.

But our hero had heard enough to make him very thoughtful. Why had Dr. Mackey been so startled to learn that Colonel Stanton was at the Ruthven plantation, and why had he been so anxious to know if he and the colonel had met?

"Here's a fresh mystery," he told himself. "I must unravel it if I can."

"I am going to return home now," said St. John presently, when the storm seemed to be clearing away. "If I don't get back, my mother will be wondering what has become of me."

"All right," answered the doctor. "But let me hear from you by to-morrow night, sure."

"I will."

"And don't mention my name to Colonel Stanton."

"But if I have him arrested you will furnish those witnesses to the fact that he is a spy?"

"I will, rest assured on the point."

A little later St. John hurried off in the darkness. Dr. Mackey watched him go, and then began to pace the floor nervously.

Jack touched Old Ben on the shoulder.

"Wot am it, Massah Jack?" whispered the faithful old negro.

"Ben, we must make the surgeon a prisoner."

"All right, Ise ready to do my share."

"I am going to jump down on his back. You follow me with the gun."

"I will, Massah Jack."

The surgeon continued to pace the floor of the cabin, and, watching his chance, Jack crawled to the edge of the loft opening.

Just as Dr. Mackey swung around on his heel our hero gave a nimble leap and landed squarely on his shoulders, sending the surgeon to his knees.

"Hi, what's this?" spluttered the rascal, and tried to throw Jack off. But our hero clung as fast as grim death.

"It means that you are now my prisoner, Dr. Mackey."

"You!" ejaculated the astonished man. "Let me go, I say!" And he began to struggle more violently than ever.

But by this time Old Ben was on the floor, and the negro lost no time in poking the muzzle of the gun under the surgeon's nose. This brought Dr. Mackey to a standstill, and he glared at his opponents in amazement.

"Don't—don't shoot!" he gasped.

"Then keep quiet."

"How did you escape from the cave?"

"That is our business, Dr. Mackey. Will you submit, or not?"

"I suppose I'll have to submit. You are three to one." Columbus Washington was now beside Ben.

"Columbus, see if you can find a rope or a strap. We'll bind his hands behind him," went on Jack.

"What are you going to do with me?" questioned the surgeon anxiously.

"Put you where you deserve to be—behind the bars," was our hero's quiet, but firm, answer.

CHAPTER XXXI.

FATHER AND SON—CONCLUSION.

"Jack, do you mean to say you would put your own father in prison?" asked Dr. Mackey reproachfully, after Old Ben had tied his hands behind him.

"I would—were he such a fraud and villain as you, Dr. Mackey," was our hero's calm reply. "You will never make me believe that any of your blood flows in my veins."

"Then you believe I am an impostor?"

"I do."

The doctor fell back and sank on a bench. Jack's firm manner appeared to take his nerve from him.

"What shall you do next?" he asked finally.

"Take you straight to our plantation."

"No! no! Colonel—" Dr. Mackey stopped short. "Do not take me there, I beg of you!"

"But I shall take you there, and what is more, I am going to find out what Colonel Stanton has to say concerning you."

At this the surgeon grew as pale as death.

"You—have no right to take me to the plantation. Remember, I am a Confederate officer. If you keep me a prisoner, you will be liable to heavy punishment."

"We'll risk it." Jack turned to Columbus Washington. "See if the rain is letting up."

The colored man went out and presently reported that the worst of the storm seemed over.

"Then we will start," said Jack. "Now, Dr. Mackey, if you try to escape, I will order Old Ben to fire at you."

"You are very hard on your father."

"If you call me your son again, I will knock you down where you stand."

At this curt threat the surgeon relapsed into silence, his brow showing plainly that he was in deep thought. The cabin was soon left behind, and Columbus Washington showed the most direct route to the Ruthven plantation. Jack came behind the colored man, with Dr. Mackey beside him, and Old Ben brought up the rear, his gun ready to shoot at the first sign of opposition upon the prisoner's part.

The first streaks of dawn were beginning to show themselves when the party of four came in sight of the mansion. As they came closer Dr. Mackey showed increased alarm over the situation.

"Jack, let us come to terms," he said presently.

"What terms?"

"For reasons of my own I do not wish to visit Mrs. Ruthven's house while Colonel Stanton is under her roof."

"Surely you are not afraid of a sick man, even if he is a Yankee spy."

At this the surgeon winced.

"It is not that. I—I—"

"I will not listen to you. March!"

"But, Jack—"

"March, I say, or Old Ben shall fire on you."

With something resembling a groan the surgeon went on, and in a few minutes more the party gained the piazza, and Jack was using the big knocker on the door lustily.

"Who is there?" came from an upper window, and then Mrs. Ruthven uttered a cry of joy. "Jack!"

"Yes, mother; I am back again; safe and sound," he answered.

Mrs. Ruthven was soon down and let him in. She was naturally startled to behold Dr. Mackey, especially as a prisoner.

"What can this mean?" she began, and then looked at Jack curiously. "Jack, do you know the truth?"

"What truth, mother?"

"That this man is an impostor."

"I have thought so all along. But what do you know of this?"

"Colonel Stanton is here, Jack. He knows Dr. Mackey only too well."

"So I supposed from what this fellow said."

"To you?"

"No, to St. John."

"My dear Mrs. Ruthven, this is all a dreadful mistake," burst in the surgeon. "I do not know Colonel Stanton at all. I spoke of a Colonel Stanwood—quite a different person, I can assure you."

"I do not believe you, Dr. Mackey," answered Mrs. Ruthven emphatically.

"You are very hard upon me, madam."

"I think I have a right to be hard upon you, sir. You have tried your best to rob me of my son."

"But he shan't do it, mother," put in Jack warmly.

"No, Jack, he'll never be able to do that—now," answered Mrs. Ruthven significantly. And then she added, "See to it, Ben, that he does not get away. I wish to speak to Jack in private."

"He shan't git away from Old Ben, nohow," answered the

faithful negro.

Mrs. Ruthven led Jack into the parlor and closed the door carefully.

"My boy, I have a great surprise for you," she began. "Do you think you can bear it?"

"What surprise, mother?" he asked quickly.

"Colonel Stanton is here, wounded. He has told me something of his past, and it concerns you."

"Me?"

"Yes, Jack. You are not Dr. Mackey's son at all, but the son of the colonel."

"I am Colonel Stanton's son!" gasped our hero, hardly able to frame the words.

"I knew you would be amazed. But it is true, as he has proved beyond the shadow of a doubt."

"But—but—" Jack tried to go on, but words failed him. He the son of the colonel—the son of a Yankee officer? It was something of which he had never dreamed. Yet, even on the instant, he remembered how much the colonel had impressed him, and what a gentleman he had thought the officer.

"I will tell you the story," went on Mrs. Ruthven, and did so. Jack was all attention, and when he learned the true depth of Dr. Mackey's villainy his eyes flashed fire.

"Now I understand why he didn't wish to meet Colonel Stanton face to face," he said. "No wonder he is afraid."

"Your father is sleeping now," continued Mrs. Ruthven. "He is improved, but still somewhat weak. You can go to him when he awakens. I think it will be best, for the present, to keep the fact of Dr. Mackey's capture a secret."

"You are right, mother."

The matter was talked over, and Dr. Mackey was later on taken to a garret room and tied fast to an old four-poster bedstead, a piece of furniture weighing considerably over a hundred pounds. Then Old Ben was placed at the door to watch him.

Just before the colonel awoke Jack went in to see him. As our hero looked at that handsome face his heart beat rapidly. He bent over and kissed the colonel's forehead, and this awoke the wounded man.

"Jack, my son!" murmured the colonel, as his eyes rested on the face of the youth. "My son, at last!"

"Father!" was the only word Jack could utter, but, oh, how much it meant! Then he caught his parent by both hands, and for a moment there was utter silence.

"I was so afraid something had happened to you," went on the colonel. "Oh, Jack! you do not know how glad I am that we have found one another!"

"And I am glad, too," replied our hero. "Do you know I was drawn to you from the first time I saw you?" he added.

"And I was drawn to you—even though you were a little Confederate," and the colonel smiled.

"And you are a Yankee!" cried Jack. "But I don't care what you are, father," he continued hastily. "Blood is thicker than water; isn't it?"

"Yes, Jack; and what is more, I trust this cruel war will soon be over, and we will have no North and no South, but just one country."

Jack remained with his parent for over an hour, then went off to see what could be done with Dr. Mackey.

It was the middle of the forenoon when Marion discovered St. John coming, accompanied by several Confederate soldiers.

"He has come to arrest my father," said Jack. "But he shan't do it."

"He will be surprised when we show him Dr. Mackey as a prisoner," returned Marion.

She went to let her cousin in, and St. John began at once to speak of Colonel Stanton.

"He is a spy," said the spendthrift. "You should be ashamed to harbor him in your house. These men will place him under arrest."

"I don't think they will," put in Jack, as he came forward. "So you are here to do Dr. Mackey's dirty work, are you," he added.

"Eh? What—er—do you mean?" stammered St. John.

"You are found out, St. John," said Mrs. Ruthven, coming on the scene. "And let me tell you that hereafter it will be best for you to remain away from this place. You schemed to steal some of my things, but you shall not do it."

"Why, Aunt Alice—" he began.

"It is true. Do you know that Dr. Mackey is a prisoner?"

At these words St. John fell back and grew very pale.

"A prisoner, did you say?" he faltered.

"Yes. He has plotted against not only Jack and myself, but also against the Federal officer who is under my roof, badly wounded."

"You mean Colonel Stanton?"

"I do."

"He is a spy, aunt."

"He is nothing of the sort. He is a brave officer, and as such deserves the best of treatment. St. John, the less you mix up in this affair the better it will be for you."

A stormy scene followed, and St. John came out of it considerably frightened, especially when he was told that the colonel was Jack's father and that Dr. Mackey was proved to be a thorough villain.

"I—I won't ask for this arrest just now," he said, to the men he had brought along. "We will let the matter drop for the present. The man is too sick to be moved, anyway." And soon after he hurried away, and his companions with him. He never showed himself at his aunt's door again.

"And we are well rid of him," said Marion. "He is as cowardly as he is unprincipled."

On the day following Jack's return home there was a long-drawn battle in the mountains between the Federal troops and the guerrillas, which resulted in the killing off of a number of the outlaws, including those who had held our hero a prisoner. In this contest Gendron was also killed, and he died without revealing what he knew of Dr. Mackey's past.

The outlaws' camp was thoroughly searched, and here were found the goods stolen from the trader who had been attacked in the storm, and also a number of other things of value, including the tin box taken from the wreck of the *Nautilus*. Later on this box, with its contents, was turned over to Colonel Stanton.

"My precious papers!" said the officer to Jack, as he looked them over. "My son, nothing now stands between us and our fortune."

A few words more and we will bring this tale to a close.

Colonel Stanton's recovery was slow, and by the time he got around again the great Civil War was a thing of the past. For this the colonel was truly thankful, and so were Jack, Mrs. Ruthven, and Marion.

As soon as it was possible to do so, the colonel resigned from the army. This done, he set to work to prosecute Dr. Mackey and recover the fortune due himself and Jack. As a result of these movements Dr. Mackey received a term of ten years in prison, and inside of a year the Stantons, father and son, came into possession of a fortune worth a hundred and fifteen thousand dollars.

Colonel Stanton had thought at first to go back to the North and settle down, but Mrs. Ruthven hated to part with Jack, and it was decided that all should remain at the plantation. A year later the colonel married the widow, so that Mrs. Ruthven, now Mrs. Stanton, became once more Jack's mother.

"And that is just what I wanted," said Jack, after the wedding.

The ceremony at the plantation was a double one, for at the time Mrs. Ruthven married the colonel Marion gave her heart into the keeping of Dr. Harry Powell, who had now set up a lucrative practice for himself in Philadelphia. The double wedding was a grand affair, and was the talk of the neighborhood for a long time afterward. The Ruthvens from the other plantation were invited, but while Mrs. Mary Ruthven came, St. John was conspicuous by his absence.

St. John was now a worse spendthrift than ever, and it was not long before the plantation went under the hammer, and Mrs. Mary Ruthven was compelled to live upon her sister-in-law's charity. St. John drifted to New Orleans and finally to the West, and that was the last heard of him. Let us trust that he saw the error of his ways and turned over a new leaf.

As for Jack, he proved to be indeed the son of a soldier, for some years later he entered West Point Military Academy, and graduated with high honors. From the Academy he, too, went West, but as an officer at one of the well-known forts. His career here was full of daring and honor, and he speedily rose to the position of colonel, which he filled with all of his old-time bravery and loyalty.

THE END

www.ingramcontent.com/pod-product-compliance
Lightning Source LLC
Chambersburg PA
CBHW030343310726
48979CB00001B/170

* 9 7 8 0 8 0 9 5 0 1 7 9 3 *